Paul Scott was born in  army from 1940 to 1946, demobilization he worked years before joining a fi resigned his directorship concentrate on his own writing. He wrote thirteen distinguished novels, including the famous 'Raj Quartet', and also reviewed books for *The Times*, the *Guardian*, the *Daily Telegraph* and *Country Life*. He adapted several of his novels for radio and television.

In 1963 Paul Scott was elected a Fellow of the Royal Society of Literature and in 1972 he was the winner of the *Yorkshire Post* Fiction Award for the third volume of the 'Raj Quartet', *The Towers of Silence*. In 1977 *Staying On* won the Booker Prize for Fiction.

Paul Scott died in 1978.

By the same author

The Raj Quartet

PAUL SCOTT

The Mark of the Warrior

PANTHER
Granada Publishing

Panther Books
Granada Publishing Ltd
8 Grafton Street, London W1X 3LA

Published by Panther Books 1979
Reprinted 1979, 1985

Originally published by Eyre & Spottiswoode
Reissued by William Heinemann in 1967

Copyright © Paul Scott 1958

ISBN 0-586-04864-2

Printed and bound in Great Britain by
Collins, Glasgow

Set in Monotype Plantin

To Penny
with all my love

Contents

This is a work of fiction and the characters are all imaginary. Care has been taken to ensure, so far as this is possible, that no coincidence of name and employment exists between the characters in the book and officers and non-commissioned officers who were actually on the staff of an officers' training school in India, or officer-cadets who trained at such a school during the period in which the action takes place. I am indebted to, and here thank, officers of the War Office and Commonwealth Relations Office who assisted me in my task.

The Mark of the Warrior

Three things are to be considered:
a man's estimate of himself,
the face he presents to the world,
the estimate of that man made by other men.
Combined they form an aspect of truth.

An Action as Prologue
May 1942

AN ACTION AS PROLOGUE

May, 1942

An Action as Prologue

THE PLAN had been to cross the river at first light, but it was well into the morning before the head of the column reached the bank and dropped exhausted. The river was deep, swollen by the rains, at this point its pace comparatively slow. But the rain was falling again and it was reasonable to suppose that by the end of the day the water would have risen further and increased in velocity. It was not a time for delay.

The column, the remnants of an Indian rifle company, was led by its commander, Major Craig. There were a surviving subaltern, two havildars, a naik and thirty sepoys: a total strength of thirty-five. Of the sepoys ten were non-swimmers. Heavy equipment had been thrown away along the general line of retreat. Each man carried a weapon, ammunition, a water-bottle, a twenty-four-hour ration of food. The general stores (the remaining rations, ammunition and two coils of manilla rope) were borne on two bamboo stretchers. The column had lost contact with its parent battalion a week before and with the Japanese four days ago. They were moving in a north-westerly direction towards Imphal across the grain of the hills of Upper Burma.

The river which faced them was not the first they had crossed. Craig said, "We'll cross now. Same routine."

Behind them, astride their line of approach, six men and an NCO already guarded the rear, spread fanwise, each watching a sector of jungle. Craig moved back and spoke to the NCO in Urdu.

"We are crossing the river now. I will call you when it is your turn."

The NCO moved his head to show that he understood.

Craig returned to the bank.

The subaltern gestured. "Me?"

"No. As before. You get on with the raft. But see I'm covered."

Craig stripped and looped one end of the coils of manilla around his shoulder. A sepoy stood guard over the coil to pay it out and secure the loose end.

Craig slithered down the bank, lowered himself into the water cautiously, leaned into it and struck out. He paused in midstream to test the strength of the current, then swam on, concentrating on his breathing. The water stung the cuts and sores on his body, the rope dragged. He reached the far bank and after a brief rest chose a tree with a stout trunk and lashed the rope round it. Then he swam back.

The two bamboo stretchers were now roped together and thus formed a raft. New poles had been cut to reinforce it.

The subaltern said, "It's fixed." He was taking off his boots. Behind him a dozen men, strong swimmers, followed suit.

Craig said, "Don't use the rope unless you're in trouble, John."

"Right." The subaltern turned round and repeated the order.

Boots strung by the laces round their necks, rifles across their shoulders, they took to the water one by one in line ahead and swam upstream of the rope. They reached the other side, sat on the bank, put on their boots. Craig watched them. The subaltern rose, called the names of six men. These he led into the jungle. The other six stayed on the bank to haul the raft and cover the crossing.

At this point there were twelve men and one officer on the far bank. On Craig's bank there were seven men in the jungle and fourteen by the river. Of the fourteen only four could swim. It was these four who dragged the raft to the water, secured the rope to its bow, went in with it to steady it while five of the non-swimmers loaded it with part of the stores and their own equipment. The other five took the second coil of manilla and lashed it to the raft's stern.

Craig said, "Right. Don't get on to the raft. Hang on."

He signalled to the men on the opposite bank. They lay to the rope and pulled. The raft moved into the stream, flanked

6

by the swimmers. The non-swimmers grasped the stern and kicked with their legs. The five men on Craig's bank belayed the end of the second rope to a tree and stood by it.

When the men and stores were safely landed on the other shore Craig signalled again and the raft was drawn back. Only two swimmers accompanied it this time. The other two went to a point fifty yards downstream and stood prepared to dive in to intercept any non-swimmer who was swept away.

. As the raft came in on its return journey one of the men hauling on the rope relaxed his hold and moved away. Craig who had watched him, said, "What is the matter?"

The man shook his head.

Craig moved to him, touched his shoulder.

"This thing is all right. You have done it before. You will be safe."

The man returned to the raft with Craig. Squatting, he undid his bootlaces while Craig watched.

The raft was loaded. With the other non-swimmers the man plunged into the water and secured a hold on the stern. The men on the far bank pulled on the rope; the raft moved. Craig was alone. In a moment he would call to the rearguard so that they could help him to haul the raft back for the last time. Then they would cross together, brew up and move on. Meanwhile he hept his eye on the man who had panicked.

In midstream the raft disintegrated. The weight of water and the stress of the rope had loosened the lashings. Poles broke free, swirled, bobbed to the current and flowed away with it. Craig plunged in and swam stiffly towards the struggling men. To those in the water the sound of firing was an inexplicable part of the catastrophe. To the subaltern and his advance party in the jungle the cries from the river indicated an attack in greater strength than that which now actually faced them in the shape of an enemy patrol of six.

Themselves misjudging the situation, the enemy patrol withdrew with the loss of one man the subaltern had shot, but in the short engagement the subaltern received a mortal wound. Two of his men, believing themselves surrounded, had fled into the jungle and of the four who had stood two were dead.

In the river Craig had saved the man who had funked the

7

crossing. The other four non-swimmers were drowned, together with one of the swimmers. Five rifles, two boxes of .303 ammunition and that proportion of the column's rations which had been on the raft, completed the tally of loss.

Later, the rearguard made its way across with the aid of ropes and the crossing was completed by 1200 hours. A rough stretcher was made and, carrying the subaltern on this, the column moved away from the river, not wanting its back to it. The going was tough and slow. At 1700 hours they bivouacked, and the rain which had fallen all day ceased.

The subaltern had borne pain stoically, but now he slipped into unconsciousness and Craig stayed with him until he died. At first light they buried him, struck camp and moved on towards India.

PART ONE: THE FOREST

January to April, 1943

Ramsay (1)

POONA WAS a place. The railway from Bombay passed through it. Their train stopped at it and was shunted to a siding where a thin scarecrow of a boy offered them his younger sister and then, having pointed her out to them and been told to bring her back in ten years when they would either be dead, back home or in need of her, proposed his elder sister who went with soldiers since four years. How much? He looked at their epaulettes. The white strips showed that they were better than ordinary soldiers but not yet as good as officers; for an officer-cadet, eight rupees. They worked it out, unused to the calculations because they had been in India only twenty-four hours. Twelve bob. No sale.

They did not stay long in the siding: four hours by Ramsay's watch, or twelve by Lawson's, which had stopped in Cape Town. They drank tea, watched each other for signs of cholera. Lawson decided that Poona looked like Clapham Junction with palms. From Poona they travelled by narrow-gauge railway to the east and then to the north-east, for a day, a night and part of the next day: one hundred cadets from England, uncomfortable, suspicious, appalled, fascinated. The landscape seemed very ordinary until thought back on; then it was odd. But that oddness, Ramsay decided, looking at it again, was in the people who had bare feet and skinny brown legs and turbans, all the things in fact which he had expected: all the things except one—an appropriate landscape against which to move.

It was a time not of disappointment but of reassessment. Ramsay had formed, for instance, a picture of the Officers' Training School for which they were bound. There was a lot of sunlight and a lot of shade from very green foliage. Framed by the foliage was a building, and this was white and ornamental outside, dark and cool within. The parade ground, somehow, was a lawn. The real picture, when it unfolded, did so piecemeal, so that again disappointment was avoided, cushioned by mild surprise and a sense of discovery.

The cadets arrived in trucks which had met them at the station with the promptness reserved by the army for transporting men into a new and possibly disagreeable experience. They debussed in a tarmac-laid square which was flanked on three sides by flower beds. There were some full-grown trees with thick boles and branches rather sparsely leaved, a flag-pole flying the Union Jack, the pole set in a bed of stones coloured red and white and laid in patterns, and a low L-shaped building sporting a verandah along its longer side. This turned out to be the mess, bar and ante-room. On the other side of the square, across the main road, red-brick buildings were partly revealed in the gaps between the thick-boled trees.

The day was grey, the expected sun quite hidden. The officer who received them explained that there was some unseasonable rain. The khaki of his well-starched uniform was lighter than that of their own tropical kit. The officer's skin was pale, not tanned as they would have expected, and the shape of his topee made them realize that their own were ridiculously old-fashioned; confirmed them, indeed, in their suspicion that the Army had supplied them from stocks originally laid down in the South African war.

They had arrived in the middle of the afternoon and about the school there was an emptiness. They sat in the long ante-room, smoked, read the unfamiliar newspapers and magazines, looked at the map of India which showed the country in much greater topographical detail than any they had yet seen, traced their route and were surprised at how little of the sub-continent they had covered. At four o'clock the receiving officer conducted them to the mess, a high-roofed, white-distempered hall partitioned into sub-messes, and in one of these they ate a meal served by Indians in white-cotton, bunchy uniforms, nipped in at the waist by wide embroidered belts. The servants had bare feet. The food, like the day, was grey, but coloured by hunger and the unaccustomed luxury of decent plates and knives with bone handles.

The word went round: We're Sahibs now.

The picture unfolded further. The mess, the central square, were on the top of a flattened hill which was cut by the main road from the school to the cantonment and the station. Back along the road, but unnoticed on the journey, they could see a row of square, white-stuccoed buildings with no upper storey but high, pointed roofs which swept down to form a verandah at the front, a narrower verandah at the back. These, the officer told them, were the administrative offices. Beyond them was the red-brick guardroom and the gateway through which their lorries must have passed. An Indian sepoy stood there, at ease, a stick under his arm, a turban on his head. It surprised them, although it should not have done, that the turban was khaki. A turban, to be a turban at all, should be white, or green, or red, like those they had seen on the way. Beyond the gate the road was lost in trees and shadow.

But on the other side of the hill, down which they now straggled from the mess, the country opened. The road narrowed and flung gravel pathways right and left into the hillocky fields where, ugly and squat, the long huts which housed the cadets stood in formations imposed not by the builder but by the contours of the ground. They moved to the farthest south of these and, as they approached, men in civilian clothes who had obviously been waiting for them clambered to their feet.

"These chaps are your personal servants," the receiving officer explained. "Each hut is divided into a dozen suites. You go two to a suite and get one servant with it."

The draft had long since paired off. Ramsay would be with Lawson. They had hut number 12 and their servant's name was Abdul. Lawson thought this comforting though dull. Abdul was short, his face was pitted with smallpox scars which gave him not a villainous but a curiously innocent, even childish appearance. He wore thin grey trousers, a white shirt outside them, a brown jacket buttoned tightly at the waist so that the shirt flared out a bit, and a brown fur cap. He spoke no English.

By signs he conveyed to them that baths were ready.

In the sitting-room on which the glass-paned door opened

directly there were two desks, two upright chairs, two easy chairs, a table, a spotted mirror. The walls were distempered cream. The inner door led to the bedroom. The beds were made. Mosquito nets bunched from the ceiling. Between the beds was a wicker table and a wicker chair for each man. The door led into the bath-house. The floor of this was concrete and sloped to a hole in the outer wall. Two galvanized iron baths were half-filled with warm water. In one corner stood a washstand with a marble top, two china hand-basins, two aluminium soap-racks. The door led out to the back of the hut and, to the left, was the latrine.

"Look at this, Bob," Lawson said. "Just for you and me." Along the back of the block other cadets had made similar discoveries. Their raised voices were full of the pride of ownership.

Behind the hut was a stretch of rough, uncut grass. Bushes formed a hedge. The hill sloped away from the hedge, and its trough could not be seen. But, beyond, the land lay in folds covered in a grass of a green which Ramsay now knew was a green he did not know because a fiercer rain, a stronger sun, a drier dust, had stained its pigment. He stood in the doorway of his and Lawson's hut and saw that the sky had no colour he recognized and that the shape of the land was not a shape which he understood in his bones. He became aware of a scent in which there was mixed the scent of smoke from fires he had not seen and the tang of earth he had not touched; and when the breeze moved there was in it the breath of men he had not met; and his blood stirred.

It was then that he saw on the south horizon the strangely shaped hills which erupted from the undulating plain. They were unlike any hills he knew. Lawson nudged him, asked, "What are you staring at?" and he pointed at the hills and said, "There. Over there. The jungle."

After tea, which their servants prepared, a sergeant introduced himself. He addressed them as 'Gentlemen' and told them to address him as 'Staff'. Yes, Staff; no, Staff; thank you, Staff. Odd.

They were D Company. They would form three platoons, numbered ten, eleven and twelve. The course started on Monday and would last for six months. There were three other companies in the school, senior to them: A Company—the members of which would shortly pass out, full-fledged sub-alterns—B and C Companies. In course of time their own Company, D Company, would become senior company. Until then, and after then, they would watch their step. They would be all right if they paid attention, tried hard and watched their step. If they failed to watch their step they would be RTU. Returned to unit. But not to England: to Deolali. And in Deolali you got the Doollalli taps because the life of a BOR in India was a chastening and mortification of the soul. What was a BOR? A British Other Rank. He was a BOR. A BOR played ball. A cadet could play ball. His name was Shaw, but you called him Staff. The Commandant's name was Lieutenant-Colonel Manville, which was French for man about town. Only a colonel could be a man about town. Beyond the cantonment was the native town. To go into the town was to take a step to Deolali. The native town was out of bounds. The contractor's daughter was out of bounds.

And what about the Commander of D Company: their company?

D Company Commander was new. He had not arrived. All that was known of him was that he had fought in Burma, was a major, would be here in a few days; and that his name was Craig.

Craig (1)

AT 1500 hours he was due to give his introductory address to the Company in the main lecture room. Esther lay, half asleep, watching Hussein adjust the buckle of his belt.

"Are you nervous, Colin?" she said.

"I don't know. I expect so."

Hussien stood back and Craig turned round so that she could see him properly.

"Will I do?"

"You need a pull on the right side. That's better. Now you'll do very well."

He bent to kiss her. She smiled sleepily, rested a hand on his arm. "What time for tea?" she asked.

"Oh, five. Five should be safe."

"Hear that, Hussein? Chae, panch baje."

"You'll sleep till then?"

She nodded, closed her eyes.

As he went she called out, "Be nice to them. I expect they're very young."

Hussein followed him to the front door. The bungalow was still strange to them and Craig guessed that Hussein would not settle until he and Esther proved by some small gesture that the newness had worn off and that it was accepted as home. The small gesture could not be invented, it had to be involuntary. Hussein had been their servant for the ten years of their marriage and could distinguish between cheerfulness and contentment.

The bungalow, of white stucco, stood in an overgrown garden. Esther, when describing the bungalow, had said that its shoulders were hunched. The trees bore down upon it from all sides. The semi-circular drive was narrowed by the shrubs which has invaded it. The place badly needed attention, but he was reluctant as yet to make plans. Esther understood this. Hussein understood it. He looked at his watch and calculated that he could walk it in fifteen minutes and be on time.

The road was deep in the shadows cast by the trees, but ahead, as at the end of a tunnel, the sunlight shone intensely. It caught the brass insignia on the shoulders of the sepoy on stick guard at the gate of the school. Craig, as he got nearer, transferred his cane to his left hand and felt in his pocket for his identity card. His was not yet a familiar face.

Through the gate, he walked up the flower-bordered path to his company office, but found the room empty and oppressive with stale heat. Its emptiness was not unlike a rebuke and he looked again at his watch and held it to his ear to check that it had not stopped at ten minutes to three. Its steady tick reassured him. On the Sergeant-Major's desk was the nominal roll of D Company. He picked it up and glanced at the names to which in time faces and personalities would fit. The names of men were, in themselves, nonsensical. Once you knew a man his name lost its rhythm and then, however ludicrous it sounded in itself, it became a picture instead of a sound. Anderson, Appleyard. . . . Dyson, Edwards, Everett. . . . Hazelrigg, Heighington. . . . Lawson, Lester, Martin. . . . Peters, Powell. . . . Ramsay . . .

Ramsay.

His eye rested there, then moved to the middle of the page where the initials attaching to the names stood in a column of their own.

R. W. Ramsay.

At once the name sloughed off the identity which previous association would always carry with it and resumed through its unfamiliar initials its own anonymity. Craig put the paper back on the desk.

He closed the door, walked down the path, screwed his eyes against the glare. The flag hung motionless. In the kitchen behind the cadets' mess a man was singing.

The main lecture hall, if he had remembered the Sergeant-Major's instructions correctly, was on the ground floor of Black G. Block G was down the hill and up the hill, past the cadets' living-quarters. He realized that he would be late after all. They would assume that this was deliberate. He despised show. His watch marked three o'clock and he had yet to climb the hill. He climbed it steadily, concentrated on his breathing as was natural to him in moments of physical exertion. His heart hammered a bit, but that was to be expected.

Now he could see his sergeants. They stood in a group by the main door of Block G, a large, red-brick building of the late nineteenth century. They had paraded in best KD and looked smart and capable and clean. They pinched out their cigarettes and when Craig was still twenty yards away the Sergeant-Major braced them up.

"NCOs, NCOs, shun."

Craig halted and saluted properly.

"D Company present and correct, sir."

Craig nodded. "Thank you, Sar-Major. I congratulate you on your staff. Jolly good turn out."

"Thank you, sir. Lead on, sir?"

Following the Sergeant-Major, Craig walked into the main lecture hall. The noise made by a hundred men coming to their feet was one to which he knew he must become accustomed. Going straight to the dais he stepped on to it and faced them.

At a signal from the Sergeant-Major the cadets sat down again and in a while there was the silence which he alone was expected to break.

Ramsay (2)

"I BELIEVE it's fashionable for a man in my position to display his right profile, his full face and his left profile, invite you to remark and remember them, and remind you that together they make a face you're going to see a lot of. If I were also consciously a funny man I should say: See a lot of, in fact, from the points of view of some of you, see too much of."

Cautious laughter stirred the assembly.

Ramsay heard the sound of it, heard the sound of Craig's voice, but he had not heard the words Craig spoke after Craig had turned his left shoulder round and so enabled Ramsay to identify the regiment whose name was embroidered below the crown on Craig's epaulette.

Little doubt remained. It must be Craig, the family's Craig, the Craig whose written words, 'I was with him when he died', had made the name Craig significant.

It must be that Craig, their Craig, John's Craig, and if it is that Craig, Ramsay thought, that is Craig's voice, the voice which had spoken to John and with which John had been familiar. It was the last voice which John had heard, and so Craig, speaking now, was a direct link with the dead. And yet this Craig was very much alive: a man, forty perhaps, of medium height and build, unremarkable, a man with thinning hair of indeterminable colour, a close-clipped sandy moustache to cover, perhaps, a too long upper lip; a dry scrubbed skin, and eyes which, from where Ramsay sat, looked as pale as if the sun had burnt the colour out of them.

Ramsay knew such a man; a decent, unspectacular man, grown into Ramsay's knowledge since the days of boyhood. There he was, topee off, but the marks of its brim still red on his forehead, his arms bare to just above the elbow, his throat uncovered, his knees naked like a boy's, his shorts a little longer than Ramsay, conforming to his age, thought right if a good, well-turned leg were to be shown to advantage. But above all it was the eyes he knew, or thought he knew: burnt out, colourless, like the Indian sky.

Staring at Craig he was conscious then that Craig was staring at him. He heard Craig's words. They seemed to be spoken directly to him.

"—isn't a branch of warfare I think we fully understand. I believe it is our job and particularly your job and my job here to learn to understand it, because unless we understand it we can't conduct it. I think we shall need to conduct it if we're to regain possession of Burma."

Craig's eyes had moved, continued to move, restlessly. He looked in front of Ramsay, behind him, to either side of him, then back to him and Ramsay remembered his own resemblance to his brother John and felt that Craig had seen it. The older man was at a disadvantage, and so Ramsay let his own gaze drop, concentrated hard, listened to Craig to understand what Craig was telling them.

"I'm not here as a chap who knows it all and proposes to pass his knowledge on to you. I'm here as a chap who only has one advantage over you. I have commanded a unit of an army which has been defeated in the field by an enemy you will one day have to face in positions of responsibility. Whatever our relative positions in this school, you as cadets, I as your company commander, we are here, fundamentally, to explore together the problems which need to be solved if you are to face that enemy with confidence."

But Ramsay found he could not listen to a man without looking at him and when he again looked up their eyes again met and he thought Craig hesitated. Certainly there was a pause. In it, Ramsay was aware of his own fixed expression, of

Craig's regard of it, of the possibility of this silent exchange forming a challenge he did not intend. Then he recalled that, although he knew Craig, Craig did not know him. It was not even true to say that he knew Craig. He knew the name, guessed at the identity: the rest was conjecture. The reality was himself and the man on the dais, the new land, the new experience awaiting him.

Craig spoke on and Ramsay listened. There was a simplicity in Craig to which the younger man now responded. It was, Ramsay felt, a simplicity distilled long ago, matured over years of experience, compounded of frankness and understanding and knowledge, and by these things Ramsay set store.

"That is all I think I have to say to you during this introductory lecture. It isn't my intention to lecture you again. Our association henceforward will be on a closer, more personal basis. I should like to be able to tell you to feel free to call on myself and my wife socially on Thursdays, when our bungalow will welcome you for tea. Unfortunately neither our establishment nor our ration scale is elastic enough to prepare for fifty and receive only one, or to prepare for twelve and receive twenty. We should like to entertain about ten of you each week and if you find yourselves forced to prepare a nominal roll of those willing to come on each occasion then let that be merely a secret between you. On Thursday we shall be at home from five o'clock and, weather permitting, tea will be served alfresco in the garden. We shall look forward to seeing you."

The Sergeant-Major barked them to attention and for a few seconds there was no sound other than the words Craig murmured to him as he went; and then, before Craig had quite gone, a cadet shouted, "Hear, hear!" and the assembly burst into applause. For an instant Craig hesitated, half turned to them, his face colouring, and Ramsay saw the small involuntary twitch of his cheek as a smile of pleasure was held in check, through surprise or uncertainty or a sense of military good manners, perhaps. Then, taking the Sergeant-Major in tow, Craig made his way out.

When the cadets had clattered down the short flight of steps at the back of the building—where the ground was lower than

18

at the front—and scrambled for their bicycles, Lawson said, "So that was Craig."

"Yes, that was Craig. What did you think of him?"

"That he confounded my preconceived notions of what a regular Indian Army officer was like."

They lined up with the others, by platoons, standing two deep on the left of their machines, facing the line of march. In each platoon a cadet had been appointed 'commander' for the week. In turn, these gave the order to move forward and then the signal to mount.

"Was he your Craig?" Lawson said at last.

"I think so."

Ahead of them a cadet came a cropper.

"Are you going to ask him?"

"I suppose so, if the opportunity arises." Ramsay looked at Lawson. "It's a bit bloody awkward. I can't go up and say, Were you my brother's CO? Because if he isn't it'd look like arse-licking."

"But if he notices your name and *he* has to ask *you* he'd think you were afraid to speak up."

Ramsay grinned back at him and Lawson added, "As you say. A bit bloody awkward."

"I could always pretend I didn't know the name of John's CO."

"It's a bit feeble."

"And of course he wrote to my parents."

Lawson said, "This one's initial is C."

"I know. I think that was it."

"Write home and check."

"I'd better do that."

They dismounted in the hut lines. Abdul stood at the entrance to number 12 and wheeled their cycles round to the back. Tea was ready.

Ramsay said, "You be mother."

"Here then."

Sergeant Shaw looked in.

"Mr. Ramsay?"

"Yes, Staff?"

"Major Craig wants to see you."

"Right away?"

"He didn't say so. He sent me to tell you he wants to see you."

Shaw went.

Lawson lifted his narrow face from his tea cup, said, "It's *your* Craig."

Ramsay, faced with certainty, nodded. "It looks like it." He glanced at Lawson, troubled.

"Don't be an ass, Bob," Lawson said. "It's worse for him if you're who he thinks you are."

It was this that Ramsay liked about Lawson; this that had drawn him to Lawson out of one hundred men.

After the Sergeant-Major had left Ramsay alone with Craig in D Company office, Craig invited him to sit down. Closer to him, Ramsay saw how near to the surface of his skin his bones lay; how the skin itself was dried up.

Craig said, "This is a personal thing, Ramsay." Then: "Are you a relation of John Ramsay?"

"Yes, sir. He was my brother."

"It was I who wrote to his parents—your parents."

"I know. They were very grateful. It meant a lot to them."

Craig looked away, reached for a tin of cigarettes on the desk and offered them. As Ramsay took one Craig continued: "I was looking through the nominal roll before I went to Block G this afternoon and noticed your name. I didn't wholly connect it with John until I saw you. You look very much like him."

"He was taller and a bit darker."

Craig nodded, smiled. "But these are superficial differences. Thanks." He bent to Ramsay's proffered light. "It's a coincidence our both turning up here, but, as you'll find, the Army is fundamentally a tight-knit community. What seems to be a coincidence is mostly the effect of the military law of averages."

Ramsay, feeling an obligation, said, "When I heard your name I wondered, of course. But I wasn't sure until you walked into the hall and I saw the regimental flash."

Craig's bony hand strayed to his shoulder, fingered the flash. "Of course."

"Actually, I wasn't really sure until you sent for me."

"I thought we ought to be certain," Craig said. He leaned back. "Tell me about yourself, Ramsay." He pushed an ash-tray across.

"There isn't much, sir. I joined last April, did six months in the ranks, went to pre-Octu. Then we came out here. That took nearly three months. We were held up six weeks in Cape Town."

"How old are you?"

"Nineteen, sir."

"Then John was quite a bit your senior."

"Yes. Six years roughly."

"Did you volunteer for India?"

"Yes, sir."

"Do you like it now that you've come?"

"I think so. It's a bit early to say."

"A bit homesick?"

"Sometimes."

They fell silent. Ramsay said, "You've been out quite a time I suppose, sir?"

"Eighteen years."

Craig stubbed out his cigarette and they both stood up.

"Look," Craig said, "this isn't really the place to talk about John—that is, if you want to talk about him."

Ramsay hesitated. He was not sure.

Craig said, "The thing is that if we don't talk about him you and I will never be able to look at each other without thinking about him. I think that would be a mistake. Come round for a drink before dinner tonight."

"Thank you, sir."

"About seven. You go out of the main gate and straight on down the road. It's number eight on the right-hand side."

"Right, sir."

Ramsay cycled back. Lawson was lowering his lanky body into the bath.

"Well?"

"It's Craig."

"Short and sweet, wasn't it?"

"He's asked me round to his bungalow for a drink before dinner."

"I shall enjoy living in your reflected glory." Lawson smiled. "I'm only joking. Do you want to go?"

Ramsay knew now. "Not really."

"But he wanted to talk?"

"Yes."

Ramsay went back to the bedroom and began to undress. Clean, starched slacks and tunic lay on the bed. His best brown shoes shone like conkers. Everything was orderly, disciplined.

As yet he was unused to the short twilight. By the time he reached Craig's bungalow he really needed the oil-lamp lighted on his bicycle. He steered the machine carefully round the gravel drive, guided by the light from the building. There was a cycle rack below the verandah. He parked his machine, stood back, looked at the open entrance with its light of welcome and knew he must invade its emptiness. He went up the steps, looked for a bell to ring. He smelt the increasingly familiar smell of mustiness which came from wood and leather. Moths and insects he could not identify danced round the ornamental lantern which hung from the roof of the porch.

He sang out, "Hello!" The sound having died the silence was heavier to him, but cutting into it came a woman's voice and then a man's. This was a home. The Army stopped where he stood, on the threshold.

An Englishman appeared, a civilian with a face similar to Craig's but a bearing which went with the house and the woman's voice. It was, of course, Craig, but, as Ramsay had often found when meeting people for a second time or for the first time against their own background, a man not entirely identical to the image Ramsay had carried with him from their first meeting.

"Come in, Ramsay. Hussein's round the back, I expect. Did you ring the bell?"

"No, I couldn't find one."

"This is it."

22

Craig held up a round brass object with patterns cut into its surface. For all Ramsay would have known it could have been something to do with burning incense. Craig replaced it on the wooden tray. "It comes from Benares. Benares Benares, not Birmingham Benares. The tray is teak."

To Ramsay the word teak conjured up a picture of elephants hauling logs of it through jungle clearings. He put his finger on the tray to feel its smoothness. On the wall above the table hung a picture: a line-drawing of a mounted man charging a pig. Next to it there was another picture of the same man standing knee high in long grass (elephant grass?) aiming a gun at a springing tiger. This was the fable.

"They're not good pictures," Craig said, behind his shoulder, "the man's holding his gun wrong."

Ramsay said, "Yes," at once regretted it because he did not really know in what way the gun was wrongly held. He thought Craig implied lack of expertise in grip and stance, but then Craig added, "He'll miss that tiger by a yard," and Ramsay knew that Craig only meant the artist's perspective was wrong, that the aim was depicted badly. He looked at it closely again and saw that Craig was right.

"I like them, though," Craig said. And so did Ramsay. It was the spirit of them and what they stood for. The pictures, the bell fashioned out of brass in Benares, and the teak tray were part of Craig's possessions, tokens of himself. Ramsay turned to him, conscious of privilege and of the necessity of not taking advantage of it.

He followed Craig from the vestibule into the main entrance hall, which was square and bare of furniture other than a dark red and blue carpet. In each of the three walls there was a door: that to their right was open and Ramsay heard the sound of a woman's high-heeled shoes, the rustle of a long dress. Craig entered ahead of him, said, "Here's Mr Ramsay, Esther."

He had expected an older-looking woman, one who would conform with his notion of Craig's wife. She seemed to him quite young, barely in her thirties. He took the hand she offered him and noticed that she had freckles upon her cheeks. He thought these attractive.

"What will you drink, Ramsay?" Craig said. "We have a

rather bad whisky and quite a decent gin. Esther and I always drink gimlets."

Mrs Craig said, "A gimlet is a gin with lime juice. I believe gin and lime's a vulgar drink at home, but we all drink it here. The lime's good for you."

She sat down. Ramsay stood until Craig had finished serving the drinks. She wore a long dress of a vivid green which Ramsay believed would be called emerald. The dress was a bit old-fashioned, he thought, because the shoulder straps were wide. But she looked well in it. The artificial light shone on her dark hair and revealed in it the deep warmth of auburn.

Now, as he and Craig sat, Ramsay consciously memorized the room. It was not, he believed, a room he would get to know well, but he felt he would look back to it. He had his drink in his hand and sat, on terms of equality, with this man and this woman, the brother of John Ramsay. He had adult identity.

It was a pleasant room. The lighting mellowed the cream-distempered walls and shone on the polished floor. Upon this floor, colourful islands, were white rugs made of a material which looked like rough, thick felt; into the felt bold patterns had been embroidered in reds and orange, greens and blues. At the windows, which kept the darkness at bay, hung chintz curtains, a homely, English touch like the three-piece suite, dressed in plain loose covers, in position in front of the empty fireplace.

The sofa was placed at right angles to the fireplace and Esther sat at one end of it, facing Ramsay. Craig sat in the other armchair, his legs thrust out, crossed at the ankles. On his feet he wore leather sandals. It crossed Ramsay's mind that Craig had put on civilian clothes for his benefit.

Mrs Craig said, "Colin was right. You're very like your brother."

"You knew him too?"

"Yes. I was a camp follower."

Craig said, "My wife was with us in Rangoon before the balloon went up."

"And after it went up," she reminded him.

She was smiling. Craig smiled back at her, said to Ramsay, "We had a job to get rid of her. My wife is a very tenacious

24

woman. We did get rid of her in time, but she was waiting for us in Imphal when we got back. She'd organized a group of women to do voluntary work in the hospital."

Mrs Craig laughed. "They wouldn't let me nurse *him*, though. They sent him up to Shillong and kept me in Imphal."

Ramsay said, "Were you wounded, sir?"

"No. I got a bit of dysentery."

Mrs Craig said, "A bit of dysentery, a spot of malaria. I thought you'd got a bit of everything the jungle could give you."

"That's why it was better to send me to Shillong. They didn't think I'd be safe with you treating me for things I hadn't got."

Ramsay said, "Were you in hospital long, sir?"

"Oh, a few months. These tropical things take time."

Ramsay nodded. A few months. John was killed at the end of May. It was probably not until the middle of June that Craig reached India and that was only six months ago. It was in July that Craig's letter had come. In it he had said nothing of himself. In this light Craig looked perfectly fit, but Ramsay remembered the Craig he'd talked to in the office and a new idea of Craig was formed; of an unfit Craig, a Craig diminished by months of illness.

He rose to his feet because Craig's wife had risen. She held out her hand. "I know you both want to have a talk about John, so I'll leave you together."

Again their hands met. In her eyes there was kindness and, because he now knew more about her, he looked for signs of the tenacity Craig had spoken of. Character was moulded in features, so people said. But he was not adept at interpreting them. There was no feature in Esther Craig's face which alone gave him the clue to her determination; there was only the whole of it, which was pretty, her expression of friendly interest and his scant knowledge of what she had done in Imphal and Rangoon: together these represented her. She had become, in these things, part of the developing pattern of his understanding of the world in which he must make his way.

"Let me get you another drink."

Craig took his glass.

Ramsay said, knowing it to be an acceptable compliment to the woman who had just left them, "This is a comfortable room, isn't it, sir?"

"Oh, that's Esther's hand. We've only been here a few days, but she came down ahead of me and got it all organized. None of it's ours, of course, except the knick-knacks and the curtains, I think. Oh, and the rugs."

Ramsay took the refilled glass.

One of us had to kick off, he thought.

They both stood, sipping their gimlets. Craig said, "My wife told me this invitation was a mistake because talking about John was the last thing you'd want to do, Ramsay. Was she right?"

"Well, no. I mean, as you said, if we don't talk about it——"

He left the sentence unfinished.

"The fact is, Ramsay, I suppose, like all chaps who lose men under their command, I can't help blaming myself a bit for John's death."

Ramsay's face felt like a mask. He watched Craig's own face, but that looked like a mask too. He said, finally, "I'm sure you've no need to blame yourself, sir."

Craig said, "Thank you, Ramsay. I don't know your parents, but of course John spoke in general terms of his family. I gained the impression of a happy one. It's not easy to escape a sense of responsibility."

"What actually happened?"

"We were crossing a river. What was left of us was crossing a river. We'd done it before and got it down to a drill. I swam over with the first rope while John supervised the construction of the raft. Then he crossed first with an advance party to keep the coast clear on the other side, while I saw the non-swimmers and the rearguard over."

Craig motioned to him to sit. Ramsay did so, but Craig remained standing.

"Most of the men were pretty near out on their feet. We'd been cut off from the battalion and had been slogging it for a week. There were one or two chaps near breaking-point and I had to keep a special eye on them."

Ramsay waited.

"What I think I failed in, Ramsay, was keeping an eye on John. When there are thirty-odd sepoys and only a couple of British officers it's not difficult to think of the other chap—the other officer—as, well, a duplicate of yourself. We'd sort of divided responsibility. It was all a drill."

Again Craig paused.

"Anyway, John went over and we started the raft crossings. The raft fell to pieces on its second crossing and at that moment John was shot up by a patrol. It was all a bit of a mess, Ramsay. We lost five men in the river and John lost four out of his six sepoys. He got one of the Japs, but he was very badly hurt. We did what we could for him. It wasn't much. I'm afraid he had a bad time."

Ramsay no longer looked at Craig, but at the table-lamp behind the sofa.

"We got him away from the river and marched on a bit. Then we settled down in the jungle for the night. He'd been conscious all the time until then.

Craig seemed to have come to the end of his story. Ramsay said, "Was it that night, or the next day?"

"That night."

Ramsay could only picture darkness, stars, tall trees in silhouette: that night, John's night.

"Did he say anything—I mean, anything you can remember?"

Craig hesitated.

"He asked to be put down."

"Put down?"

"The stretcher. He asked to be left."

"Left in the jungle?"

"Yes. He knew he'd be holding us up."

A wave of coldness broke over Ramsay's shoulders.

"But he said nothing else?"

"Yes, Ramsay. He asked me to finish him off."

Ramsay, after a moment, said, "He was in great pain, then?"

"He had a stomach wound."

Stomach. A man wounded in the stomach knew great thirst, but could not be given water. So he understood. Perhaps it was not true. He said, "I'm glad you've told me." He was

27

glad. He was glad that *he* had been told. He was glad that Craig had not written this thing to his parents. Knowledge of John's suffering was a seal on the secrecy of brotherhood.

At last Craig sat down. Ramsay watched him, returned the grave smile.

"And I'm glad I've told you. What I haven't explained fully, though, is this feeling I can't escape from of being responsible. He must have been dog-tired and I ought to have seen it. He bodged the raft. If I'd done my job I'd have run an eye over it. Then I'd have seen it. And if I'd seen it I'd have known he wasn't himself. If I'd seen he wasn't himself I don't think I'd have sent him over first. But of course I did send him over first and he ran into the patrol.

"That's another thing, Ramsay. I think that when he got to the other side he was so weary he just let the men bunch up. They'd all had it and he hadn't the resources left to do anything about it. They were sitting ducks."

Ramsay said, "But those things add up to something else, too, don't they, sir?"

"What?"

"That John was killed through his own——"

Again he left a sentence unfinished. The right word escaped him. Carelessness, thoughtlessness, incompetence. These were harsh words, wrong words. He had kept his eyes on Craig, and hoped for Craig to find the word, but Craig found no word. Instead he stared back.

Ramsay tried again. "I mean that John had only himself to blame."

"In the last resort we rely on our commanding officer."

Craig rose. "Let me give you one more drink." He held out his hand for Ramsay's glass.

"Two's really my limit, sir."

"A weak one, then."

Craig's shoulders bent over the table at which he dispensed the drinks. He returned to Ramsay, gave him his glass, but said nothing.

Ramsay blurted out, "It isn't really so, sir. In the last resort we have to rely on ourselves."

Craig drank before replying. "Not in the way you mean.

When a man is in command of a unit he is in command. He is responsible in the fullest sense of the word. If you had said, in the last resort a commanding officer must rely on himself, I would agree. That is what I failed to do, Ramsay. I relied not on myself but on your brother, whereas he, having come to the end of his self-reliance, should have been able to look to me. Shouldn't he?"

Ramsay thought: He's asking me. He's not sure. He's feeling for an answer I don't know.

He said, "I expect you've thought a lot about it, sir. But I don't feel John's being killed needs any explanation." He hesitated, still aware through Craig's silence that Craig had asked a question and that it had gone unanswered. "It was just bad luck really. I'm glad you've told me about it."

"I thought we ought to clear the air."

Ramsay smiled, "Yes, sir." The air was not clear. He knew it. He thought Craig knew it. But there was nothing more to say; nothing certainly that would bring John back, bring him alive into this room to tip the scale, to answer the question. For a while they talked of other things, of India, of Ramsay's first impressions of it.

"I shall have to get back, sir."

"Yes, I mustn't keep you. I'll see you to the door."

Someone had lighted the lamp on his bicycle. Craig said, "Oh, that's my chap Hussein. He's good at detail."

"Please thank him for me."

"Yes, I'll thank him."

Ramsay pulled the cycle from the rack. He thanked Craig and said good night. As he turned out of the drive he looked back and saw that Craig still stood there. With a wave of his hand Craig went in and Ramsay mounted his cycle. It was quite a pull up the hill. The night air was cool and scented. He thought of John. He said John's name aloud, and was relieved for him that it was over, that John had got through the thing he had had to get through, that it was not a continuing thing which had no end, no let up. He supposed he should be proud of his brother, for bearing pain, for meeting the logical end of a soldier, for his willingness to be left to die on the way, to be put out of his misery, shot like a sick animal

29

by a comrade. But he was not proud. He was moved by John's courage, sickened by his wound and awed by the wide, far-reaching darkness which had come at the end. This was pride, perhaps; what people meant by pride.

He got off his bicycle to push it up the last stretch of the hill. Underneath the things to which people gave familiar names there was something unexpected, something which gave the name new meaning.

Craig (2)

FOR A long time Craig lay with his eyes shut, trying to sleep. He knew that Esther had woken, disturbed by his last impatient movement, that she listened in the darkness, would go on listening until the rhythm of his breathing satisfied her that he slept. He moved his right hand, groped for contact. Her own hand, warm, comforting, touched his wrist.

"Shall I get you a drink?"

Her voice was low, level.

"No. You go to sleep. I'll be all right."

"Some hot milk?"

"No, it's all right."

She pressed his hand, held it for a moment; a gesture which meant: Stay there.

When she had gone, he opened his eyes. She had not put the light on, but a shaft came through the half-open door from the dining-room. He heard the clink of a saucepan from the kitchen beyond. Such sounds at night, when the world was asleep, comforted him. The tension in him relaxed and at once he dozed. He opened his eyes when she switched on the lamp by the bed, and watched her through the softening blur of the mosquito net. It always moved him to rediscover that deeper than duty and loyalty, and informing each, was love.

"You'll get no sleep," he said.

"Here."

He sat up and took the warm glass of milk which she handed through the net.

"Do you want an aspirin?"

"No. This'll be fine."

The clock on the bedside table showed ten minutes to two. In four hours Hussein would wake him. He would drink strong tea, shave, dress, go on the first parade. Esther would sleep on. They would meet at nine o'clock breakfast, at one o'clock lunch, at five o'clock tea. The evening would be theirs.

Esther said, "Do you feel like talking?" She sat on the bed, outside the net.

"What's up?"

"I wondered if you're sorry I talked you into taking this job."

"No. Why should I be sorry? It's better than the thing at Delhi. We'd have had no time to ourselves."

"That's true."

"You know what it's like there."

Esther said, after a moment, "I wasn't thinking so much of that, though."

"What, then?"

"Of the job itself. Coping with a lot of boys."

"They're not all as young as—as that."

He drank his milk.

She said, "Tell me about the lecture."

"I thought I did."

"You only said it went down well."

She lighted a cigarette, lifted the net and gave it to him.

"I'll want an ashtray."

"Use the glass. *How* well did it go down?"

"Pretty well." He looked at her, smiled. "They clapped."

"Clapped?"

He watched her consider this, felt her probe into his own estimate of it. He said, "Sergeant-Major Thompson didn't approve."

"Is he any good?"

"Yes. Thompson's all right."

"What's it like having British NCOs to deal with again?"

"They're on the cautious side."

"Did they like your lecture?"

"Not much."

"Why, Colin?"

He smiled at her again. "You're trying to find out what I said."

"Naturally."

He lay back, smoothed his ruffled hair with his free hand. She said. "Another time will do. You're sleepy." Now he wanted to talk, to share the day with her. He said, hurriedly, "Thompson and the NCOs didn't like it because the tone was too friendly, I suppose. But the boys saw what I was getting at."

She nodded, got up and left him to smoke the last of his cigarette while she returned to the dining-room and kitchen to check the lights. He heard the snap of a switch, the click of a door, her slippered footsteps. The cigarette fizzed in the bottom of the glass. In the morning it would be split open, the tobacco sodden and dark, the ash congealed and black.

She took the glass from him, tucked in the net.

"I'll do the light," he said.

"It's all right."

She switched it off. In a moment she was round at the other side of the bed, climbing in. Her movements were studied, quiet. She muttered sleepily, "I'm glad it was a success."

He understood. Again he reached for and found her hand. They slept.

The dream came in yet another new form. He walked up the hill, knowing it was a hill only through the strain of climbing it. The fat leaves and creepers had to be thrust aside, but every so often he was imprisoned by them and had to struggle to free himself. Then at the moment of despair came the empty plain, the white-hot sky, the dead-weight of isolation. It was in crossing the plain that the variations came. There was always the hill, always the plain, and it was never until he stood on its great empty expanse that he knew this had been dreamt before.

Sometimes, when crossing the plain, he was in company; tonight, he was alone. On the horizon the land erupted into a range of strangely formed hills, jungle-covered hills, which were blue with distance, but before he could reach them there was the swirling, broken raft, the sense of drowning which returned time after time and changed the tempo of the dream so that he could no longer say to his dreaming self: I dream; no longer escape the reality which returned like this, in sleep. The hill and the plain were the first theme, the swirling water and the broken raft were the second; a variation linked them. The theme of the water and the raft was also the pivot of the dream. From this point it took many different directions, but always directions which led to the same end. Tonight he was helped from the water by Sergeant-Major Thompson while the sergeants watched from a vantage-point beneath trees. They pinched out their cigarettes as he walked towards them. They accompanied him into Block G, but when he walked into the room he knew they had gone and the room was empty like the plain.

He turned round to ask why this was so, although he was afraid to turn because in each version of the dream he had need to turn to look for something, to ask a question, and always he would find Ramsay there; and so tonight he turned, as he was bound, and it was not Ramsay he saw, but Ramsay's young brother.

He woke, and the picture of the dream returned, pattern by pattern, like segments of a stained glass window which could not be put together comprehensibly. Here was a picture of himself climbing part of the hill; here the bobbing, broken raft; here the deserted lecture hall; here the face of young Ramsay. He closed his eyes again so that he could remember the separate patterns more vividly, but by now inanimate objects alone could properly be reconjured. People in the dream, looked back on, seemed to have been but ideas of people which had left no sharp memory of features or expression. Instead of the dream face the real face of young Ramsay remained to be considered and, thoughr his face, Ramsay himself: Ramsay and the fact of Ramsay, here, a few hours ago, alive, spoken to, listened to.

Craig thought to himself: Say it. All right, I'll say it. I am afraid of young Ramsay. I'm being ridiculous, but I'm afraid of young Ramsay. He is his brother all over again.

He turned on his side, carefully, so that he should not wake Esther. But as he lay still again he knew that she had not been

33

asleep. He wanted, then, to hide himself against her and make his confession. His body was rigid with the effort it took both to do it and not to do it. How would he say it? How would he not say it? In the end, as always, he could only say it silently into his own darkness. I was no good, Esther. After years of playing at soldiers, when it came to it, in the jungle I was no bloody good. We were none of us any good. No bloody good at all. Except Ramsay. He knew. He knew what we were doing and where we were going and why. He didn't depend on me. I depended on him.

Craig (3)

AT THE end of a week, Thompson, embattled within his professional assurance, passed judgment on the company. "They're always the same. Six months in the Army back home, they come out here and think they know it all. Young twits. Except Ramsay. He promises well. He's not like the others. He wants to learn. You can see it."

Together they cycled to the first parade. The air was still damp with the before-breakfast moisture which carried scent sharply to the nostrils. The track along which they rode wound its way through trees, past Blocks A, B and C, where stacked cycles were evidence of early morning lectures for other companies. The track, unmetalled, grew rough, its red-brown dust ribbed by the print of cycle tyres, then, where the belt of trees ended, it came abruptly on to an open area of beaten earth.

D Company, dressed in PT kit, were going over the assault course. Craig and Thompson watched them. The course began with a straight run of twenty yards to a brick wall which was about ten feet high. The first two men to reach it formed a platform with their shoulders from which elevation the next two men achieved the top and lay, stomachs down, head pointing towards head, but with a gap of some three feet between them in the middle. With one arm extended and pressed down the far side of the wall to keep a purchase on it, the other arm of each reached out to grip those of the men who followed, to give them an anchor to haul themselves up the flat face. From the other side they ran a further twenty yards to a ditch six feet wide and five feet deep. Those who did not leap it clean hauled themselves up from the pit. The next obstacle was an entanglement of barbed wire raised eighteen inches from the ground. The men crawled under it to the other side, where they were confronted by a series of pits across the middle of which were laid uneven logs, narrow enough to demand a sense of balance if the crossing were to be made without a fall. From the pits it was a race to the rope bridge: two lengths of rope, parallel, one above the other, stretched between two trees. The men climbed up the bole of the tree, set foot upon the lower rope and gripped the upper with their hands. From the tree at the other end they swung, one by one, by a rope, across another pit to a raised bank. The rope was swung back by Sergeant Shaw, who shouted mocking encouragement to the man waiting for it.

From the raised bank they ran a course of hurdles interspersed with barrels, through which they crawled. The last obstacle was a long, narrow, shallow pit, filled with water, covered by brushwood. There was enough space between the surface of the water and the overhanging brushwood for a man to raise his head and breathe. The quickest way was to take a deep breath and crawl through with the front of the face immersed. From the ducking the men emerged as though sprayed with red-brown paint from head to foot. Their singlets and shorts stuck to their bodies, indistinguishable from their stained skin except by the wrinkled folds round the legs and at the waist. In this disarray they fell in by platoons and awaited the order to dismiss. Breakfast would be served in the mess in half an hour. Baths awaited them in their huts.

Craig watched them, understood them. They were now as happy as sandboys. The muddy water dripped; their teeth and the whites of their eyes shone. There was no attempt at silence, or the discipline of parade. They waited impatiently, on their toes, ready to charge across the ground to the trees under which their bicycles were parked.

Thompson stood in front of them.

He said, "Well, gentlemen," and silence fell, because they knew instinctively that routine was to be disrupted.

Thompson, hands behind his back, rolled slightly on the balls of his feet. "A little bird tells me that our assault course here is dead easy. Nothing, for instance, like the sort of thing you're used to at home. It's come to my ears that one young gentleman is of the opinion he could go round it on his arse."

There was a shout of delighted laughter. Thompson held up his hand.

"Now which young gentleman was it?"

Someone stepped forward and Craig tried to fit a name to him, but failed.

"And what is your name, sir?"

"Lawson, Staff."

"Thank you, Mr Lawson. Fall in."

Lawson stepped back.

"Now I'm sure none of you other gentlemen think yourselves less agile than Mr Lawson here. It is a temptation, a very great temptation to get Mr Lawson to give us an exhibition of this remarkable talent. An even greater temptation to invite you all to join him in displaying it. However, I am assured by the best authorities that a wall cannot be scaled that way; authorities, I mean, better informed as to the anatominecal limitations of the human body than Mr Lawson can be at his age. It isn't, gentlemen, our job here, or our intention, to indulge in buffoonery. It is our intention to train officers. If our equipment is less advanced than what you have been used to we'll have to get our effects by working it harder."

Thompson looked at his watch.

"There is twenty-five minutes to breakfast. Ample time for energetic and efficient gentlemen like yourselves to pop round the course again, wash and dress. Move!!"

For a moment they hesitated.

"Move, I said!" Thompson shouted and, like a chorus, Sergeant Shaw yelled, "You should be there by now."

It reached Craig then as they moved, the sharp odour of resentment, and he knew that Thompson had made a mistake, but he walked over to the brick wall, to join Thompson, to give him additional authority. The cadets had begun the attack on the wall and Craig was impressed by the fierce determination with which they scaled it. They seemed, right from the beginning, to take charge, and subtly altered the technique laid down by the school for dealing with the obstacles. The wall was scaled at the double; the first man—Lawson—sprang at it, hauled himself up unaided, paused momentarily at the top to steady the man behind him before vaulting down on the other side, and so set a pattern for all to follow; a pattern which dispensed with the two men prone on the top, one which demanded of each cadet greater agility and sterner muscular effort; one which carried the cadets over the wall in record time.

Craig walked round the course, followed by Thompson. Neither of them spoke. Lawson kept his lead. When he came to the rope bridge he launched himself over rhythmically, swinging hand over hand from the lower rope only. He found it tricky to get up on to the platform in the tree, but managed it well enough. A few other men followed his example until the less athletic of them, using both ropes, yelled "Pack it in!" The jerking of the rope which they depended on for a foothold made the crossing hazardous.

Craig stationed himself on the raised bank and was there to steady Lawson as he landed. Lawson panted. Sweat, mingled with the drying mud, stained his face. He could hardly speak, but paused as if he wanted to.

Craig said, "I almost believe you could, Lawson."

Lawson, mouth open, chest heaving, stared at him, and Craig feared that the joke had misfired. And then, warming him, was Lawson's breathless grin. The cadet behind was shouting for the rope. Lawson, beating Craig to it, grabbed it and swung it, and then, turning to Craig again, he said, "He ought to have made me try."

When it was over and, dripping once more, the cadets had dashed to their bicycles, Craig walked slowly from the parade with Thompson.

He said, "I think what you did was a mistake."

"I don't know, sir. It's like this. They think they're tough. All right, I'll toughen 'em."

"Not by making them do things twice."

"I wanted to bend them. I reckon they're bent."

"I don't agree. They did it quicker and neater the second time."

"Not all of them, sir. But anyway, what do you suggest, sir? A tougher assault course?"

Craig shook his head. "No, I've never been over an assault course in my life. I rather think you've not either."

"I've been over this one, sir."

"Did it bend you?"

Thompson had the grace to smile. "A bit, sir."

"It's a question of what you're used to and the use you make of it. I don't agree with you that these chaps are young twits, as you put it. They're used to a different form of training, one that's more formidable technically."

"They think we're out of the ark because we've only got Vickers machine guns and not their precious Bren."

"That's what I mean, Sar-Major."

"In fact, sir, they sneer at everything we've got and everything we stand for. I don't mind telling you it gets my bloody goat. They get worse each draft. You'd think there'd never been a Dunkirk to hear them talk about Burma. The truth is though, sir, in one way they're right. We *are* out of date. We get the arse-end of any new equipment that's going and the training could be more practical, if you want my frank opinion."

"Practical in what way?"

"More field training, sir."

"It has to be a comprehensive course. It's set on lines laid down at GHQ."

"Yes, sir."

"You don't think much of GHQ."

"No, sir. Not if they're responsible for the course."

"How could you alter it?"

They had reached the fringe of trees and stood now near their bicycles. Thompson got out his cigarettes, offered them to Craig.

"I'd cut out all the sand-table exercises for one thing. Give them the problems on the ground."

"Sand-table exercises have a special function, though. At least they do from my point of view. Get out on the ground and dot the chaps round the landscape and you can only judge a handful of them. Get them all round the table, set a problem and pop questions at them and you see what they're up to."

"Well, that's true. But some of the model exercises would be better on the ground. Then there's the fortnight's camp at the end of the course."

"Not long enough?"

"It isn't that, sir. They always go to the wrong places. What's the good of training officers for jungle warfare if you take 'em to the sort of place A Company's going, where there's hardly a tree for miles around and they sit about digging themselves in and having set-pieces every other day. You'd think they were going to spend the rest of their careers on the North-West Frontier."

"Where do you suggest we should go?"

"To the jungle, sir."

Craig inhaled smoke. He said, "And where shall we find that?"

But he knew in which direction Thompson would point.

"Over there, sir, in the Chota Bandar. It's about thirty miles away and the going's really rough."

In the distance the eruption of hills had formed their familiar pattern out of the morning haze. They were not blue now but green; a green so dark that it seemed as though they lay in shadow.

He said, "I'll think about it. There's plenty of time."

Ramsay (3)

THEY SLOGGED on, knew thirst and the exhausting weight of equipment. A fine red dust covered their cheekbones, their noses, their chins, collected wherever the bones of their faces jutted. The unmetalled road was supported on an embankment. Below them the paddy fields were dry. A mile ahead there was shade from a cluster of trees, where large black crows circled lazily; and distantly the land folded itself into familiar shapes which showed them they were on the way back to the school.

The piercing blast of Thompson's whistle scattered them down the embankment. There, pressing their heads against the sharp stubbly grass, they waited in the deep afternoon silence for the imaginary aircraft to pass.

Ramsay closed his eyes. Someone worked the bolt of his rifle and pressed the trigger. A murmur of laughter swept up the embankment and Thompson yelled, "That man! That bloody funny man."

The whistle shrilled. All clear. Ramsay pressed himself up and scrambled back on to the road.

"Who worked his bloody bolt?"

They recognized the earnestness of Thompson's anger. A cadet stepped forward.

"Me, Staff."

"Me, Staff. Me worked my bloody bolt. You're supposed to be a gentleman. I'm the one that's not supposed to be able to talk the King's English."

"I, Staff."

"And why did you work your bolt?"

"I forgot."

"Forgot what?"

"Forgot we're not supposed to be here, Staff."

For a few seconds Thompson stared at the man. Then he said, "Be so kind as to step out in front and repeat to us the orders we're under."

The cadet did so. "For the purpose of the exercise," he said, in a harsh voice, unused yet to command, "we are a long-range penetration group in enemy country. Out objective is the culvert at a map reference given us by the IO. We are to blow this culvert—which represents a bridge. Until that is done we should do everything to avoid detection."

"Thank you, Mr Martin."

The cadet moved back into his section file.

Thompson went close to him. "What did my whistle represent?"

"The sound of approaching, low-flying aircraft."

"Then why did you fire at it?"

40

"As I said, Staff. I forgot. I don't think I'd have forgotten if it had been the real thing."

When they reached the group of trees Craig was there, resting in the saddle. The grey cropped a patch of short green grass.

"We'll have ten minutes break, Sar-Major."

They stretched out on the turf at the side of the road. Ramsay rested his head on his pack. When he took off his topee the sweat dried on his forehead and gave him an impression of coolness. Lawson asked him for a cigarette. He found and threw him a damp, twisted package.

"These are no good, Bob."

"They're all I've got. Bring your own."

Lawson lit up. He threw the package back. The smoke from the cigarettes was almost invisible in the heat.

Craig rode forward after a while and said, "The bridge you're supposed to be blowing up is actually Block G. In other words, the exercise ends there, though we've brought you a long way round to it. You might call it an introduction to the technique of route marching in tropical countries. These are conditions I need no introduction to, which explains why I've chosen to come on horseback." He paused, then added, "But if any of you fancies himself in the saddle, I'll walk the rest of the way. Hands up."

Several hands shot up. Ramsay looked at Craig through half-closed eyes and saw Craig glance at him. A cadet was selected, changed places with Craig. Ramsay thought: He's got off the horse because he knew we resented his having it easy while we slogged, but he shouldn't have got off. He should have stuck it out. He tries too hard to be liked.

Craig said, when the cadet had quietened the horse's uneasiness, "At this part of the march I propose to set a problem. It's really a very simple one. Let us suppose that you are on this approach to the culvert and arrive at this point. Let us also suppose that it is night time. Finally we shall suppose that instead of being a column you are a six-man patrol. Much to your dismay you find here a strongpoint, an enemy pillbox, well defended by a perimeter of barbed wire. You wait in absolute silence and hear the unmistakable sound of a man moving. You decide that this is the chap on guard. Later you hear snores and decide that these are from his sleeping companions. Now. That is the problem. Each of you consider yourself leader of the patrol. What would you do?"

Ramsay leaned back. It was a disappointing problem and he wondered at Craig trying it on. He knew exactly what he would do. He knew that he was right. He watched Craig nod at the cadet nearest to him.

The cadet said, "Have I any wire-cutters, sir?"

"Yes. You might presume to have wire-cutters."

"Then I'd cut the wire at the back of the pillbox, creep in and chuck a grenade through the window."

"I see. Thank you. What about you?" He nodded at a cadet farther down the line. "Do you agree with that course of action?"

"No, sir."

"Why?"

"Make too much racket, sir. I'd take my chaps in. There's only one of the enemy awake. By the time he'd let out a squawk we'd have got the rest."

"You mean with a bayonet, say?"

"Well, yes, sir."

"I see. Well, providing they don't yell you'd certainly have overcome the sound problem. What is your name?"

"Dyson, sir."

Craig looked back to the first man. "And yours?"

"Everett, sir."

Craig stroked the neck of the grey. Suddenly he turned.

"Ramsay? What do you think?"

Ramsay said at once, "I don't agree with either of those solutions, sir."

"Why not?"

"An attack wasn't necessary, sir."

"Why?"

"Our objective is the culvert. We're to avoid detection."

"What about the barbed-wire perimeter?"

"Well, it is only a perimeter. It wouldn't obstruct you."

"You'd find your way round it and do nothing to attract the attention of the chaps in the pillbox?"

"Yes, sir."

Craig nodded. "That's quite right. It's a trick question, of course. Thank you, Ramsay."

Lawson muttered, "Clever boy."

Craig (4)

COLONEL MANVILLE said, "I don't know, Craig. It would be so expensive and inconvenient. What's wrong with the area we've always used?"

Craig hesitated. Care was essential. "I don't think it would serve for the sort of field training we're aiming at."

"*We*'re aiming at? Who's we?"

They were being wary with each other, but Craig wondered whether Manville at last would face him with it, ask him what the hell it all meant. Yes. Here it came.

"I've meant to have a word before, Craig, and that rather brings me to it. *We*'re aiming at. Meaning you and your cadets are aiming at?"

"And the staff."

"But, fundamentally, you and the cadets."

Craig said, "Yes, fundamentally."

"You know, Craig, I'm *sure* that's wrong, that attitude, that idea of doing it together, working it out together."

"But then we are doing it together. We have to."

"No, no. I'm sure it's all wrong."

Manville fumbled with the neat clip of papers on his desk. He had died long ago. Only his body remained to go through the motions of administration. The man about town: Craig had heard him called that. One could see that once he might have looked the part.

Because Craig said nothing Manville repeated, "I'm sure it's all wrong."

He hates silence, Craig thought. Being dead he hates silence.

"You see what I mean, Craig?" Manville asked.

"I'm not sure that I do, sir. Except that you disapprove."

43

"Well now, it's in your mind too. I give my Company Commanders wide powers. I don't express disapproval. But my disapproval is in your mind."

"You said my method was wrong."

"Only for you to prove it right, Craig."

"How do I do that——" he began, and stopped, trapped.

"By taking your chaps into the jungle. One of us must be right. Try it. Try it. I think it's wrong. Expensive and inconvenient. But try it. Perhaps you'll do well. You know the jungle, Craig."

"No, sir. I must learn to know the jungle——"

"You've been in the jungle. God, Craig! What a barbarous place to fight a war."

"Yes, sir."

"Well, go into your jungle."

"I've not finally decided. I'll know better today when I've recced it."

"Is that what you wanted the truck for?" Manville's thin finger smoothed the top paper on the clip. It was in the papers, buried in the figures: Craig's truck.

"Yes, sir."

Manville asked, "Are you going alone?"

"No. Sergeant-Major Thompson's coming."

"And you've got a map, presumably. Get lost without a map."

"Yes, sir, I've got a map."

"Well, go into your jungle, Craig."

The truck was waiting outside his company office when he returned. Thompson also waited, spruce, alert; extra spruce, extra alert because what they were about to embark on was in the nature of a jaunt for him.

It was half past ten. They drove, Thompson at the wheel, to Craig's bungalow to pick up the hamper.

Esther greeted them.

"I wish I could come. I've just seen the tiffin Hussein's put up for you. It's made my mouth water."

Craig said, surprised to see her, "I thought you were shopping?"

"I should be, but Mrs Manville wants me for coffee at eleven. I'll shop after." She smiled at Thompson. "But I envy you both."

"It's a roughish sort of ride, Mrs Craig."

Craig waited, helpless.

Esther turned to him, "Then you've decided where you'll go?"

Craig said, "Yes. To the Chota Bandar hills."

None of them spoke until suddenly Esther said, "I must come too, Colin," turned without waiting for his reply and went indoors.

He heard Thompson say, "What about rations, sir? Shall I pop back and get something?"

"No. There'll be enough. Hussein always packs more than's necessary."

Now he looked at Thompson, observed the faint puckering of his brow which was all the sign his rank allowed him to give of his wish to say, We were *always* going to the jungle. That was always the plan. Why didn't you tell her? Why did you tell her a lie?

Esther returned with shoulder-bag and topee, stout shoes on her feet.

In the truck he turned to her where she sat on a padded bench behind them, and said, "What about Mrs Manville?"

"Hussein's taking her a note."

Thompson drove the truck out on to the road and Craig carefully unfolded the map.

They had arrived in dead ground and the hills to the south could not be seen. They had made good time. In three-quarters of an hour they had covered twenty-five miles of indifferent road.

"The bumps are to come, sir," Thompson said. The red-brown dust had already entered the truck. The sun had begun its process of beating them into the shape of travellers: arching towards its midday zenith it had taken the breath out of the morning.

The thick hair on Thompson's forearms, the sparser on his own, had darkened and lay damp and close to the skin. He clenched the hand which lay on his knee and then unclenched it because the knuckles had risen like hills. But then, re-thinking it, he clenched it again. These hills on his hand were bare, the contours familiar, unsecretive. He raised his head. The truck was climbing out of the hollow and then, once more, the jungle-clad hills of the Chota Bandar were in front of them. But the road had taken the travellers to the east and they came to the hills from the north-east, and found the shape of the hills subtly changed.

Esther said, "Oh, they *have* got a third dimension."

Craig said, "Didn't you think they had?"

"Not from back there. They've always looked like a theatre backdrop to me."

Thompson said, "Not when the sun catches them as it goes down. Gives them a sort of depth."

"I hadn't noticed that," she said. "Do you watch them at sunset, Mr Thompson?"

"Now and then."

"They are deep, though, aren't they? I mean they stretch back for miles."

Craig said, "According to the map."

He looked down at the folded linen-backed paper on his knee: a paper on which these hills were shown as an irregular patch of violet surrounded, like a dark island, by flat seas of brown and green. The road along which the truck jolted and scraped runnels of dust marched parallel with the line of hills, separated from them by a mile or two. Ahead, according to the map, it would turn to the right to avoid a long low spur, but turn left again sharply and worm its way inwards, feeling for a grip among the hills themselves.

"This road goes right through them, does it, Colin?"

Thompson answered for him. "It takes the northern valley."

"Is there a southern valley?" she asked.

"Yes, then a series of ridges and ravines," Thompson said.

"What is there in the southern valley, another road?"

Craig said, so that Thompson should not say it, "No. The river." He added, turning round to her, "Or so it's marked on the map."

46

Thompson sounded the horn at a darting black goat. They had passed through a hamlet. He said, "Dry at this time of year I expect, sir. Have to wait for the rains before it can be called a river."

Craig nodded. He was sensitive to Esther's quietness. Suddenly she broke it.

"But won't it be raining in June?"

"I expect so."

"I meant won't it be raining when you're on your field training?"

Thompson grinned. "Yes, Mrs Craig. All the better. With any luck the rains should break slap in the middle of it. A couple of weeks in these hills, a good downpour or two. It'd be the making of them."

Esther said, "But you haven't definitely decided on the hills yet. Have you, Colin?"

"No. Not yet."

"What did Colonel Manville say, sir?"

"He left it to me."

Thompson slowed for the turn. "Well," he said, "that's something. He's always been dead against it."

"I may be myself, Sar-Major."

Craig paused. Thompson said nothing. Craig added, "We'll have to see what it looks like."

Thompson glanced at him. Their eyes met. Thompson smiled; a wry, half angry, half happy smile.

"You and I know what it'll look like, sir. Like Burma."

It was then that Craig noticed something about Thompson he had failed to recognize before. In Thompson's eyes, behind his eyes, was the look he had seen in the eyes of John Ramsay —a look of wisdom, beyond his comprehending. He looked from Thompson to the map; from the map to the closing hills. Lines, colours, shapes. Meaningless.

It would be no different, after all, this time. Esther had spoken. "What did you say?" he asked.

He had swung round to her; now they stared at each other and Craig remembered the times when he had woken in the dark, crying out for her, unable to tell her why.

For a time he avoided having to climb the slope and enter the forest. The truck was drawn up on the side of the road which traversed the northern valley. Ahead, the valley broadened a little, but here, where they were parked, a spur narrowed it and the ground rose almost from the roadside. The slope had been cleared by wood-cutters. Ferns had grown amongst the stumps. On the other side of the road the slope was gentler until two hundred yards away the northern ridge rose abruptly, thickly wooded, tumbling its crest into the shapes familiar to them in reverse against the southern sky. They had come round the northern ridge by the road. The middle ridge, the watershed of the northern and southern valleys was the one they had decided to explore. On the other side of it was the river.

Esther collected the refuse of the picnic. Thompson rose to his feet, helped her, carried the backet back to the truck. When he came back to them Esther said, "You'd like to start, I expect."

Craig said, "Will the truck be safe?"

"I've immobilized it, sir."

"We ought to have brought a driver."

"Do you want me to stay?" Esther asked.

Thompson said, "It's quite safe, Mrs Craig. No one takes this road. Not the sort that'd pinch a truck, anyway."

The afternoon had settled to silence and heat and glare. Craig said, "We ought to have a plan," and Esther, who had risen, moved away a pace or two.

"I thought we'd get on top of the ridge, first. See what the going's like, sir."

"And then what?"

"Have a look at the river, sir?"

"I suppose so."

Craig paused, watched Thompson grope for a question.

"Have you got something special in mind, sir?"

"No. It just looks as if now we're here we don't know what we're looking for. Precisely looking for."

Thompson seemed to want to help. "Well. I suppose if we had a picture of the sort of scheme we want to lay on, that would be a start."

"I have no picture, Sar-Major. The hills were your idea. Have *you* a picture?"

Esther came back to them, but said nothing, stood only between them, waiting for them.

Thompson said, "No clear picture, sir. I think it'll come if we look at the ground."

Craig replied, "Then let's look at the ground."

They gathered their things together and set off. The sun struck suddenly on their necks as they left the shade of the tree under which they had rested.

Craig stopped. "You lead the way, Sar-Major," he said.

"Right, sir."

"You'd better have the map." He handed it to him.

For a while they walked together, Thompson only a pace or two ahead, but when the ground got rougher they spaced out, with Esther between them, and picked their way through the ferns and lopped branches. The slope steepened. Craig paused, turned and surveyed the road which was now below them. There was the road, the truck, the tree, the northern ridge which with its prongs enclosed the road so that within his vision the road had no beginning and no end, points only at which it was no longer visible to his eye. Within his eye was a memory of the map and he knew where the road came from and how it came, and where it went to and how it went. But this did not help him. In front of him he saw the jumble of country known as the northern ridge, and behind it, if he turned and followed after them, was the centre ridge with the river and the southern ridge beyond it. He knew the contours of the centre ridge and the contours of the southern ridge. He knew the way in which the river bed defined the line of the valley on the map. He understood these things with the eye of his memory. But this did not help him; and when he turned round and trudged after them he was a man in an unknown country.

Esther had waited for him.

"What were you doing? Planning some frightful problem for the boys?"

"Not consciously."

He looked ahead. Thompson had reached the fringe of the forest.

"Come on. The Sar-Major's waiting," he said.

They trudged the last of the scarred slope together. His heart had begun to hammer. He concentrated on the rate of his breathing. When they joined Thompson he saw that the other man showed no signs of strain. As though Craig had strength to give her, Esther leaned on him lightly, companionably, excluding Thompson from their knowledge of each other.

Thompson said, "If we strike half right we ought to come out on the highest point of the ridge and it won't be such a climb."

"No. Let's go straight ahead."

Esther agreed. "It'll be shorter."

Thompson said, "Right."

And now they entered the forest.

It was quiet at first, as though the trees of the outer fringe, standing sentinel, enforced a zone of silence in which the forest would hear the noise of men who entered it. As they invaded deeper, higher, Craig listened, tuned his ear away from the sound of their boots and shoes scraping the rough skin of the hill, until he could hear the other sound, of tree and hill quick with life and growth, a singing sound which echoed in a green dry cave.

A man's voice called, "I think we're off the track, sir."

He stopped. The corners of his eyes stung where the sweat had gathered. His head ached from the tightening band inside his topee. He took the topee off.

"Mr Thompson says we're off the track, Colin."

"Does it matter?"

His head was expanding with the relief of removing his topee. He had not seen a track. He heard Esther call, "Major Craig says don't bother," and Thompson's voice came back, "Right, but we'd better veer right a bit or we'll go straight for the dip."

But there was no dip, surely? There was only the ground rising ahead of them, the trees thickening, the roof of the cavern darkening. And then, as they marched on, following Thompson's lead, he saw to his left a thinning of the roof where the sky filtered through trees rooted lower in the ground and he was then aware of the way in which the ground plunged suddenly and darkly. They skirted the chasm and climbed steeply to the crest of the ridge.

Thompson waited for them, consulted his map. Esther sat down, licked a finger and touched it to a scratch on her leg. Craig leaned against the tree by which she sat. His heart was all that he could hear. The forest said nothing to him. Esther's voice rose above the sound of his heart, but she spoke to Thompson.

"What now?"

Then she turned to look at Craig and Thompson looked at him, and he could not get his breath to speak. Instead he mutely indicated the slope to the valley and pushed off from the tree down into the tumbling forest.

He heard Thompson call, "It should be quicker down to the left."

He caught hold of a low branch, steadied himself and turned. "Quicker?"

Thompson was above him, legs planted firm, poised. Thompson explained: "Quicker to the river."

"Don't we come to the river this way?"

"Oh, yes, we come to it, sir."

"This way then." He stared at Thompson, unwilling to catch Esther's eye. Esther waited behind Thompson.

"Do you want the map, sir?"

He shook his head, steadied himself again and began the descent.

All the life of the forest was here, between the middle and southern ridge. Esther cried, "Monkeys!" and above them the treetops were shaken by the swift passing of dark agile bodies, the air suddenly loud with their bickering. The monkeys had never been in the dream. The monkeys were a new thing, and when they had gone Craig saw that the afternoon had become twisted and savage because the three of them were scrambling down the hill, but were separated from it and from each other.

He stopped. He had come to a track. Here, people had passed; many times, back and forth, over the years, beating down the earth, thrusting a way through the forest. From which direction? With what end in view? He looked at the track and then around him. Where was the river?

Esther reached him. She said, "Which way?"

Thompson arrived, map in hand.

Craig said, "Which way? Left, isn't it?"

"Either way, sir."

"Either way?"

"Yes, look, sir." He held the map out. "We're on the main spine of the centre ridge. The river comes round in a big loop. If we went straight ahead and ignored the track we'd come out right where the river pivots. The track joins the river in each direction, on either side of the loop."

Craig looked at the map. It was quite clear. There was the part where the contours of the ridge were drawn outwards as though magnetized by the bend of the river. There was the dotted line showing the track. He looked up from the map and to the left where the track was swallowed up, and the map told him that the track continued on into the green darkness, that it veered fractionally to the right, skirted a bulging contour which indicated a fold in the hill and so came to the line of the river bed.

But this was not what the forest told him.

The river bed was dry, save for a channel of water which defined the line of its deepest course. Flood-wrack bore witness to its turbulence in past rains.

They stood on the north bank and stared at the dense jungle on the other side and the strange outline of the southern ridge, the main feature of which was a long, humped hill with, at its eastern end, a sudden rounded peak, higher than the hump, which fell away gradually on its farther slope into the lower hills.

Esther said, "Elephant Hill." She sat down. "At least we've christened a hill."

Thompson laughed. "Elephant Hill. That's good. We could make that the objective, sir. An attack on Elephant Hill. Complete with river crossing."

From behind them Esther said, "Won't that be dangerous in June?"

Craig looked at the river. "It's not very wide," he said.

52

"Not very wide, but pretty fast, Colin, when the rains have been at it."

He kept his eyes on the river and considered its treachery. On the map it was a simple black line which curved through the valley. The reality of it was different.

Thompson said, "It won't flow so fast on the other side of the spur. The water'll crowd up to the bend and only get momentum on this side. Like a traffic jam."

"But it'll be deeper."

"Probably, sir. Shall we go and look?"

Esther said, "I've had it for a bit. I'll sit and smoke."

"I'd rather not leave you alone."

"Then stay with me and Mr Thompson go."

"No. It's something I ought to look at."

"I think you should rest. You're overdoing it."

Thompson said, "You stay with Mrs Craig, sir. I'll soon nip along."

"No. I must see for myself. You look after Mrs Craig."

He walked back up the slope to the track.

"Colin!"

He paused, looked at her over his shoulder. She was getting to her feet.

"You stay," he called. "I shan't be long. There's no need for us all to come."

Again he entered the forest. It was perfectly simple. All he had to do was to follow the track, because it led to the river in both directions. For the first hundred yards he moved as quickly as he could and then, satisfied that Esther and Thompson had not followed, he slackened pace to the trudging rhythm of the infantry soldier.

He stopped to light a cigarette. Before he went on he listened. Nothing was ever silent in the world; except death, and that was at a world's end. He had held Ramsay's hand in a place like this and had watched Ramsay gather such a silence to him. And when Ramsay had gone he had continued to hold his hand because it was his link with Ramsay and Ramsay's link with him, and he had been afraid to be alone, to face the forest alone. He did not understand the forest as Ramsay understood it. This Ramsay had known. The men had felt it, and been divided by it. With Ramsay buried, a passion of sadness for them had moved him, and then they were not divided but bound to him and he to them, because Ramsay was dead in the forest and they alive in it. He had thought: We are alive in the forest. Like children they had blundered their way through it. Like children, forgetting Ramsay, they had looked to him, and soon he had borne alone the knowledge that the forest had beaten them, that they trudged on without hope of the forest. In the end the forest had relented, delivered them, and Craig saw that for them he was the forest and he the deliverer, and some had wept.

He came to the river and saw from its wider channel that Thompson was right, that here the water would flow slower. The track had widened and here, on the bank, it continued down towards the river bed. At this point, then, there was a ford in the dry season. He began to cross. Before he reached the channel, the bed softened and so he halted and looked downstream to the point where the river turned. Fifty yards away the channel widened even farther and the flow lessened. Beyond the ford, then, the water would be deep. When the rest of the river bed was all-but dry there would still be a pool there.

Standing, he had sunk a little. The muddy bed sucked at his feet as he lifted them and turned back. He knew that he experienced at this moment a reality which the dream would absorb; that, in sleep, he would turn like this, imprisoned in mud, and find Ramsay. He paused, said aloud, "But which Ramsay?" for the dream employed its own cunning and had revitalized the expected shock of turning to Ramsay by ringing the changes on the two brothers. Which Ramsay?

He climbed the bank, slipped, dirtied his clothing. He would have to face the others and they would say, Did you fall? Yes, he would say, I fell, but it was nothing: I went down into the river bed and, coming back, I fell. And there would be a picture for them of a man losing his balance. The thing which had happened here, now, would enact itself again in their minds. When they saw him they would see the evidence of his fall. The forest divided them, but the track linked them, and knowledge of accidents linked them, and none of them was alone. Hang on to that. If he shouted they might hear his voice far off. If they started along the track to meet him his voice would be nearer.

He got to his feet and stood on the top of the bank. He did not know whether they had decided to meet him and were already walking along the track. If, going back, he met them, then he would know and be able to reconstruct their moment of decision. One of them, Esther more likely, would have said, "Let us go and meet him." Thompson would help her up and then, together, they would set out along the track. When they met he would know this had happened and they would know that he had fallen and the forest would yield up its secrets of them.

Ten yards within the forest there was a break in the track. The track forked in two directions. He couldn't remember seeing another track come in to join the one by which he had walked to the river. For a while he stayed at the junction and considered the way each track went. One track was the wrong track. The one going to the left was the wrong track. He walked a little way along the track which branched to the right, turned, and considered the view, tried to recall whether this was the view he had seen when approaching the river. Surely this track was moving too abruptly to the right? If so, where was it leading?

He thought of the river and of the way it looped round. The track he was on probably led to the bend and in that case it was the other track he wanted. He returned to the junction and noticed how easily the existence of the other track could be missed. He walked along the other track, turned, considered the view. There was not really any difference between the view from one track and the view from the other. He walked on a little way.

He could see his way perhaps ten yards ahead. At the end of the ten yards a further ten yards. The forest revealed itself section by section. It was like the dream remembered on waking in each of the isolated pictures, which only sleep and the sub-conscious mind could combine; that or the forest wisdom of a man like John Ramsay.

He halted. The track was wrong. It was climbing the hill.

He retraced his steps, looked for the junction, missed it and came out again by the river. The trees and the earth and the water were etched sharply in sunlight. He felt that his eyes had no depth. He sat down, lighted himself a cigarette. He knew now which track to take. He was quite safe. He could even go round by the bed of the river itself or move through the edge of the forest by the bank of the river. Between himself, Esther, and Thompson, there was a lifeline, the twin strands of the track and the river bed. The forest divided them, but it contained them.

Then he thought: If I go by the river bed and they've decided to meet me on the track I shall miss them. The thought nagged. It would be all right if everyone stayed still until he had completed his own action. He told himself: You want them to stay by the river. You want to go by the river bed in order to be sure. You are afraid of the track and of the way it might deceive you.

He threw his cigarette away, half-smoked, and got to his feet. He had wasted enough time. At the junction of the two tracks he hesitated and then set foot firmly on the track leading to the right. He had no faith in it. He could only rely on the surer evidence the other track had given him of being the wrong track. No part of the forest he now walked through was familiar, and, having set out on it, he believed it likely that Thompson would expect him to recce the whole river bed round the loop and so come that way: that Thompson, expecting this, would have gone that way to meet him. If that were so, then at this minute the three of them were in different parts of the forest without knowledge of each other's actions. He wished to draw the three of them together, protectively, warmly, humanly.

Quite suddenly the track dipped and he saw the rippling water of the channel in the river bed and then the glowing colour of Esther's hair where she sat in the shade, reading the map. The sound of his coming escaped her. She sat quite still, and he felt for her the sharp, small stab of love which accompanied reunion. As he approached he saw Thompson standing down near the river bed, shading his eyes against the sun which shone over Elephant Hill.

Esther had not heard him, and she was nearer, but Thompson heard him. Thompson swung round and on his face Craig saw an expression which stopped him in his tracks. Everything became clear.

"Go and judge for yourself," he told Thompson. "There's a basin below the ford and it's deep."

"Right, sir. But you think it'll do?"

Craig said, "Oh, yes. It would do."

"What about Elephant Hill, sir?"

"Elephant Hill?"

"I mean, can you see it from behind the spur?"

"I'm sorry. I didn't notice. Why?"

"I thought that it was a point to check, sir. If troops dug in on Elephant Hill could see that section of river."

Craig said, "Well, you check. I think a river-crossing there would be in dead ground to chaps on the hill. But you check it."

Thompson scrambled up the bank.

Craig called after him, "Come back along the river bed. See how it goes. We'll wait for you here."

"Right, sir."

Craig waited until Thompson was out of sight. Then he climbed back to where Esther sat.

He said, "May I talk?"

She gazed at the river bed. "Yes, Colin."

He sat down by her. He had no need to touch her, no need of her touch. He said, "You've been very patient, Esther."

"That's the least of the qualities I should show for you."

He took out his cigarettes. When he offered one to her she hesitated and then accepted it. He lit her cigarette, his own, and said, "You knew I was afraid of the jungle, didn't you?"

"I wasn't sure. I thought it might be something else."

"Such as?"

"Something preying on your mind, like John Ramsay's death."

He said, "There was that too. But that wasn't the main thing."

"Has something happened?"

57

"Yes."

"To make you not afraid of the jungle?"

"I think so."

He looked at her. She still watched the river. She said, "How were you afraid of it, Colin?"

He hesitated.

She said, turning to him, "Don't say, if you'd rather not. I don't *have* to know. What I know or don't know can't actually help. That's why I've been what you call patient ever since you came back. I count myself lucky that at least you came back. All I've really hoped is that our being together might help in the end."

"I think I'd like to tell you."

"Then tell me, Colin. I *want* to know. It's just that I don't *have* to know."

He said, "I can explain it better if I tell you what's happened."

She nodded.

He leaned forward a little, tugged at the lace of his boot. "When I was in the forest just now I thought of you sitting here and of Thompson somewhere else, probably coming to meet me, or both of you coming to meet me, and our missing each other. I wanted to draw us all together so that we'd be safe. Then I came out of the forest and saw you and that was two of us safe. Then I saw Thompson."

He caught her eye. Now that he was about to speak of it the idea became a fire inside him and he saw his excitement communicate itself to her. "Then I saw Thompson," he repeated. "I saw Thompson properly for the first time. You remember —you didn't hear me coming. He was down in the river bed, and *did* hear me coming. When he looked round I saw that he was alone in the forest and wanted to be alone in the forest because he was in the forest *to kill*."

He smiled. "Whereas I and most of the men I remember were in the forest to live."

She said, "Most of the men?"

"Yes. Except John Ramsay. He was in the forest in Thompson's way. It's like a mark on them."

"Them?"

"Men like Thompson. And Ramsay. It was strong on Ramsay."

"You said he was the finest soldier you'd ever known."

"He was. They are. The rest of us are nothing. The rest of us are dressed for the part."

She watched the river again.

He said, "Once I thought I had a vocation, Esther."

"You're a good officer."

"Average."

"The men were very fond of you," she said.

"I was fond of them."

"Isn't that something?"

"Something, yes. We wanted to live, we were afraid of the forest and of the enemy. What we all wanted and what we were afraid of linked us together."

"They liked you better than they liked Ramsay. I saw that much in Rangoon."

"They liked me but followed Ramsay. When Ramsay was dead they had to follow me."

"You brought them out safely, Colin."

"Ramsay would have done it in half the time, at half the cost. And what sort of soldiering is it to have staggered out of Burma, chased by the Japanese?"

She stubbed out her cigarette in the ground. She said, "You wish you were like Ramsay or Thompson?"

"No. But I'm supposed to be a soldier. I ought to be like them."

"I'd hate you to be like Thompson."

"Forget Thompson then. Take Ramsay alone——"

"—or Ramsay."

"—all right. I'm not joking, Esther."

"I know you're not."

"Thompson has the mark. Ramsay had it, but he was an intelligent man. Thompson's intelligence is limited. Perhaps you wouldn't like me to be like Ramsay, perhaps I'd hate to be like him myself, but I have seen Ramsay and I've seen myself and what I am in relation to him as a soldier is third-rate. Now do you see?"

"Yes, I see, Colin. I don't agree with you, but I see."

Craig stood up. For a while he said nothing. Then: "You don't see. I want you to see, Esther."

She rose.

He said, "We'll go to meet Thompson."

He took her arm and helped her up the slope into the forest.

"But he's coming back by the river," she said.

He repeated, "We'll go to meet Thompson." He led her for a few yards along the track and then turned and entered the jungle of trunks and roots and undergrowth. After several paces he stopped, turned to her.

"Listen," he said. He could hear her breathing.

"And look." He watched her as she turned her head to the left and to the right and then, almost involuntarily, upwards. "And behind," he said.

He led her forward again. They came to the edge of the forest, which grew right up to the bank of the river bed down which Thompson would come.

"What did you see and hear?" he asked her.

"I heard a parrot, the sounds we made breaking through. And I saw the forest."

"What did you imagine you saw and heard?"

"Are you serious?"

"Yes."

"I thought Thompson was watching us."

"Why?"

"I don't know why."

"Because he *might* have come back through the jungle?"

"Yes, he might have."

Craig smiled at her. "And thinking he might be in the jungle you thought he was watching us?"

"I suppose so. I always get the feeling of being watched in a place like this."

"That's because you're afraid of what might be in the forest. You want to survive. You're on the alert."

"Isn't that a virtue?"

"For people like ourselves. We were on the alert, but our being alert wouldn't have enabled us to see Thompson if he'd been there and was deliberately hiding from us. Whereas,

60

Esther, if we had been deliberately hiding from Thompson he would have sensed it."

"I don't believe it."

"He would have sensed it. John Ramsay would. You're forgetting that I've seen John in a forest like this. I expected every tree to hide an enemy. Only he *knew* when the enemy was there."

"A sixth sense?"

"Of the man who is not in the forest to survive but to kill."

"He senses his quarry?"

"Yes, Esther. Such a man senses his quarry."

"And you think Thompson is such a man?"

"I know Thompson is such a man."

"Put it to the test, Colin. Here. Now. Put it to the test."

Craig moistened his lips. "That's what I've brought you here to do." He took her arm. He felt its stiffness. Esther was afraid.

"Kneel down here, as if you were going to fire at him."

"He'll never see me here."

"No."

"Then——"

"He won't need to *see* you. I'll kneel behind you." He took up his position. "And be very quiet."

From where they knelt they could see through the screen of foliage thirty yards up the river bed. Behind them, through the silence and stillness, they heard the movement of the forest.

She spoke in a whisper, "He won't know we're here, Colin," and from the way she said it he knew that she wanted Thompson to know they were there because this was something in which her husband had put his faith. He watched the back of her neck and noticed the way in which her hair curled up from it and he said silently, "Esther, Esther." She tensed. He looked up and saw Thompson coming towards them, picking his way carefully over the river bed.

As Thompson moved he turned his eyes continuously to the opposite bank. Once he stopped and referred to the map which he still carried, turned it, orientated it to the lie of the land. Now he came forward. Below the place where they were concealed the bank sloped steeply and he would pass within twenty feet of them and a little below them.

Ten yards away he paused and began to take out a cigarette. Then, before he had brought it to his lips, he again hesitated and seemed to listen. Slowly he placed the cigarette between his lips. He struck a match, lighted the cigarette and spun the match away. He walked forward, towards them. Now he was level with them, passing them. He stopped. Very slowly he turned his head towards the bank and looked into the forest. Eventually his eyes rested on the place where they knelt. For a moment Craig thought he had actually seen them and was about to challenge them. For several seconds Thompson stared deliberately into the forest. Then he moved on.

When they could no longer see him Craig stood and helped Esther to her feet. As they walked back through the forest she said, "You told me once that John asked you to finish him off."

"Yes, he did."

"Did you finish him off, Colin?"

"No, Esther." He took her hand so that she would know better that he spoke the truth.

She said, "And John's brother? Has he got the mark? Has he got the killer-instinct, too?"

"I don't know." But I do know, he thought. That's what I must first have recognized in him. That's why I was afraid of him. I mustn't be afraid. I need young Ramsay. We all need Ramsay, men like Ramsay.

Ramsay (4)

LAWSON SAID, "Surely you've noticed it?"

"Noticed what?"

"The way Craig's always looking at you?"

Ramsay broke bread. "No, I haven't noticed." He put a piece of the bread on his plate and used it to mop up the last of the bacon and egg.

Lawson said, "You don't notice people. You only notice things. You're not human any more."

"Thanks."

They had had the Chinese restaurant to themselves, but now two cadets clattered up the stairs and greeted them, sat down at the next table—the one in the corner. Ramsay and Lawson were by the window and could look down on to the main street of the cantonment bazaar, illuminated by the light from the restaurant and the naphtha lamps in the open shop fronts.

"What's good?" one of the cadets called.

Lawson said, "Bacon and egg."

"It says here fly rice."

"What *is* chop suey?"

Charlie came in, grinned at them, switched at the table cloth with his napkin.

"Bacon and egg, Charlie."

"Bacon and egg twice?"

"Twice."

Charlie went.

The other cadet said, "Everett's got jaundice."

Lawson asked, "Have you seen him?"

"Just come from there. He's had it for a fortnight but didn't dare say in case he was put back."

Lawson nodded. "How long will he be in hospital?"

"Three weeks, I expect. The week's holiday'll save him going to a junior company. He'll only miss a fortnight."

"Who was at Craig's bun-fight today?" Lawson asked.

One of the cadets ticked off the names on his fingers.

"That's twice that old Lester's been."

"Says he fancies Mrs Craig."

"More likely Craig's arse."

Ramsay stirred his coffee. There was a short silence. One of the cadets broke it.

"You been to one of their tea-parties yet, Lawson?"

Lawson shook his head. "No, I'm waiting until young Ramsay here will go with me."

"I thought you'd been, Ramsay."

"No, I haven't."

"I thought you were the first," the other cadet said.

"You're wrong. I've never been to Craig's for tea."

Ramsay watched them. He saw the way in which they caught each other's eye, the way in which they were confused when they saw that he had seen.

"You'd better get your finger out then, Ramsay. They say old Craig keeps a list."

The other said, "No, it's Mrs Craig that keeps the list."

"D'you think old Craig satisfies her?"

Ramsay turned his head. Lawson was watching him.

Ramsay said, "Shall we go?"

"I want more coffee. There's no hurry."

"What do you think, Ramsay?" one of them said.

"Think about what?"

"Mrs Craig."

"Don't ask Ramsay. He's not interested in women. He's only interested in soldiering."

"I thought a woman could be soldiered. Come on, Ramsay. You're supposed to be an intelligent bloke. What's your opinion of Mrs Craig? Don't you think she'd soldier well?"

"You'd better ask Craig."

"Perhaps Craig doesn't know the whole story. You know what these regimental wives are."

"More coffee, please, Charlie," Lawson said.

"Two more coffees?"

Ramsay nodded. For a while he watched the people in the street below.

"He hasn't brought the bread. Hey, Charlie! What about some roti? Roti lao aur jeldi karo."

"Charlie doesn't speak Urdu."

"I'm glad you recognized it. We're in the presence of experts."

Lawson said, "Expert. Not experts. Ramsay here's the expert."

"Is it true that your munshi's got you on to script already, Ramsay?"

"Yes, it's true."

"Old Ramsay's something of a wonder boy. He'll be top cadet of the course. You see."

"Pity they don't hand out swords these days. I'd like to see

Craig hang a sword round his waist and kiss him on both cheeks."

"Oh!"

"I bet it'll be Ramsay's scheme Craig's going to choose for the final camp."

"You submitted a scheme yet, Ramsay?"

Ramsay said, "No, not yet."

"Cooking up something special?"

The other cadet said, "Why d'you think Craig asked us to submit ideas for the camp scheme?"

Lawson said, "Perhaps he can't make up his mind what to do with us."

Charlie brought their coffee. It was lukewarm. They drank it quickly.

"You chaps going to the pictures?" one of the cadets asked, finishing his bacon and eggs.

"What about it, Bob?" Lawson asked.

Ramsay looked at his watch. "All right."

"Can we make the second house?"

"Just."

"Come on then."

"What about coffee?"

"Have a nimbo there."

They went down the stairs. The young Chinese clerk reckoned their bill on his abacus. At the door one of the cadets punched Ramsay lightly in the back. "Only a mild mickey, Ramsay."

The four of them cycled to the Majestic.

Craig was there with his wife. Officers and cadets sat at the back of the hall on a raised platform. The roof was pointed and of corrugated iron, but there were splendours too, an electric sign outside, a tiled foyer, modern lamp brackets on the distempered walls of the auditorium, two projectors. Ramsay believed he had seen the film before.

In the interval after the news, the trailer and the Three Stooges comedy, Craig was not to be avoided.

"Hello, Ramsay. You remember Ramsay, Esther."

"How are you, Mr Ramsay?"

65

"Fine, thank you, Mrs Craig."

"Esther, you've not met Lawson, have you?"

Later Mrs Craig turned to him again.

"Are you looking forward to the week's break?"

"Yes, I am. I think we all are."

"What are you going to do?"

"I'm not sure. But I'd like to get out a bit."

"Get out where?"

"Into the countryside."

She smiled. "I thought that after all the schemes and route marching you'd be fed up with the countryside."

"No. I meant farther afield. But you can't get far on a bicycle on these roads." His eye wandered from her to Lawson. He had felt Lawson's watching, and Craig's watching and the watching of the two cadets who had made up the pictures foursome.

Mrs Craig said, "Where would you go, Mr Ramsay?"

"To the Chota Bandar."

"Why there?"

He looked back at her. "I can see it from the back of my hut."

The bell rang. The door leading into the auditorium opened. Mrs Craig raised her voice a little, to be heard over the noise that came from the audience.

"The local bus goes within five miles of it."

Craig said to her, taking her arm, "We'd better go back in."

Ramsay stood aside for them.

When the picture had been running for ten minutes he said to Lawson, "I've seen it before."

"So have I."

"Let's go, then."

One of the cadets said, "You two off?"

"Yes."

The foyer was empty, the box-office closed. Light shone from the cinema on to the deserted road. They found and unlocked their cycles.

Lawson said, "Damn. I've got a flat."

"Push it then. We'll walk."

They set off in the direction of the school. A moon had come up.

"Why d'you want to go into the jungle, Bob?"

"To see it."

"Obviously. What else?"

"Nothing else."

Lawson's questions irritated him. He had locked these things away from Lawson.

Lawson said, after a minute or so, "Why aren't you enjoying the course, Bob?"

"Why do you think I'm *not* enjoying it?"

"You ought to be enjoying it. You're so bloody clever. I didn't think you were a clever type. It's not very comfortable living with a clever type."

"You can always move into Everett's room."

Lawson hesitated, then, "No. I shall move into Lester's room. He had nobody with him and nobody likes him. I don't like him either. I like you, but I can't quarrel with you. I shall be able to quarrel nicely with Lester."

Lawson moved that night. When he had gone Ramsay faced loneliness. He looked at this loneliness closely and found that it was one of the things he had wanted.

There was one other thing that he wanted, but he did not know its nature. Lawson's going brought it, he felt, nearer. Lawson had cleared the deck by going. He faced his loneliness and he faced himself. He looked at his reflection in a mirror and said, "Face yourself, Ramsay."

The self which he faced was thinner. His cheekbones showed. His resemblance to John had strengthened. The mirror was like a window, through which John watched him and spoke to him: It began when Lawson said to you: Clever boy, and when, silently, the others echoed Clever boy . . . There was nothing clever about you, but they said Clever boy, and you were free of the herd and looking for something which Craig knows is in you to find.

Lawson said that Craig watches you and you said that you had not noticed. That was a lie. Craig watches you all the time. Craig hasn't rejected you. He wanted you to escape the herd and yet in most ways Craig is one of the herd himself. Only in this other way, in not rejecting you, in watching you, does he identify himself with you and not with them. It is as if Craig has seen in you something you have yet to find. Now that Lawson has gone you will find it.

On two occasions Craig had chosen him to lead the company as Cadet Commander on the tactical schemes they performed over the open country south of the school. He knew the land and the sky which flattened the colour out of it, and once when he sent in a two-prong attack on a bare hill-feature and watched his colleagues worm their way through cover to the start-point his stomach had knotted with excitement at the thought of the hill and of the men who helped him to impose his will upon it by force of arms.

The hill had been swarmed over, adjudged taken by the umpires: the position consolidated. The magic had gone out of the afternoon by the time he had trudged down the forward slope of the hill, victorious, with Thompson saying, "Well done, Mr Ramsay," and Craig at the bottom of the hill, where the cadets fell out, saying, "Good show, Ramsay."

Well done. Good show. Clever boy.

He sat with the blank paper on the desk in front of him. He had drafted three schemes. He had torn them up without submitting them. On to the blank paper his mind projected images of the country he knew. Here was a road, unmetalled, the earth of it ground by the sun into dust as soft as velvet. The road ran straight. In the distance there were hills and trees, but these were far. This was tank country, a place for swift decisive movement forward. Now the image changed. Here was the bare hill, men charging up its slope.

Sergeant-Major Thompson knocked and entered.

"May I come in, Mr Ramsay?"

Ramsay stood. "Come in, Staff."

"Am I interrupting?"

"Of course not." He offered Thompson a cigarette.

Quite soon Thompson came to the point. "We believe you're working on a scheme for the field training fortnight at the end of the course."

"Yes, Staff."

"We wondered about it, you see. Frankly, Mr Ramsay, none of those we've had are any good. We've been expecting one from you."

"I'd like to submit one."

"Well, don't be too long about it. These schemes take a bit of laying on. Especially if we're going to organize some Indian troops to take part."

"I didn't know that was visualized, Staff."

Thompson nodded. "I suggested it to Major Craig. We could get them if the scheme's good enough. There'll be a battalion of sepoys in training camp about twenty miles from here in May and June. We think we could get a company to come along. It would help them and help us. But the scheme's got to be good." Thompson paused. "How long's your scheme going to take to put down on paper?"

"The putting down is the least of the troubles, Staff."

"You mean you've not thought it out yet?"

"I've thought out three, but they weren't right."

"What was wrong with them?"

"I'm not sure. They didn't seem right to me."

"Can you analyse that at all, Mr Ramsay, why they didn't seem right?"

Ramsay watched Thompson closely, saw that Thompson was pumping him. "Yes, Staff. They were static. Whatever I planned to get movement into them they stayed static. Turned themselves into set pieces."

"What made them static?"

"The ground."

"The ground?"

"The ground round here. It's not infantry country. It's tank country. I want a scheme that's infantry all the way along. One that has its roots in the idea of infantry."

"We can't alter the ground."

"No."

Thompson said, "We've always had quite decent local schemes."

"But the ground is wrong, Staff."

"Suppose it was the real thing. Suppose we *were* fighting over this ground."

"It would be static. Either that or one side would sweep the other away. Bust its way through with tanks. The infantry would mop up, or dig in. Obviously any sort of ground can be fought over, but the fighting alters its character with the character of the ground."

Thompson smiled. He had rarely seen Thompson smile. It was a cold smile. Ramsay felt that he understood it.

"What sort of ground is what you'd call infantry ground?"

"Where you can't take your tanks or your lorries or your carriers."

"Where is that, Mr Ramsay?"

"Into the jungle."

"That's not wholly true."

"Hill jungle. Where you just slog it out."

"Have you been in the jungle?"

"No."

For a while Thompson said nothing: then, "Would you like to have a look at the jungle, Mr Ramsay?"

"Yes, Staff."

Thompson stubbed his cigarette. "Have you spoken of this to anyone?"

"At the pictures the other night. Mrs Craig asked me what I planned to do next week, when we're off duty."

"And you said you wanted to go into the jungle?"

"Yes, Staff."

"To the Chota Bandar?"

"Yes."

Thompson smiled again. "How would you get to the Chota Bandar?"

Ramsay said, "She said the local bus went within five miles of it."

"She?"

"Mrs Craig."

"Of course." Thompson paused. "You were talking to Mrs Craig?"

"Yes."

"So Major Craig doesn't know you want to go to the Chota Bandar?"

Ramsay flushed. He looked down at his hands. "But he was there. He heard."

"Why are you blushing?"

Ramsay grinned to banish the heat from his cheeks. "I thought it was laid on."

"Thought what was laid on?"

"This talk."

"This talk? Me with you?"

"Yes."

"Laid on by whom?"

Ramsay let the grin go. "By Major Craig," he said.

They held each other's eye. Thompson said, "I don't know what you mean, Mr Ramsay. Laid on by Major Craig? Why would Major Craig lay on for me to talk to you?"

"I thought he had put two and two together, Staff."

Thompson made an impatient gesture. "Talk straight, Mr Ramsay."

"All right, Staff. He's been waiting for me to produce a scheme. That much you admit. He heard me mention the Chota Bandar and guesses I'm thinking of a scheme there. Since it's a competition it would be wrong if he appeared personally to make it possible for me to go there and recce, so he's asked you to check with me."

Thompson had taken out his cigarettes. He held the packet half open and then looked up at Ramsay. "That's very interesting."

"You mean it's not true?"

"No, it isn't true."

"Then I apologize, Staff."

"No need." He held out a single cigarette for Ramsay, then selected one for himself. He leaned forward to the match which Ramsay offered. "Yes," he repeated. "Untrue, but very interesting. And only partly untrue, Mr Ramsay. Major Craig has said nothing to me about believing you planned a scheme in the Chota Bandar, and nothing to me about having a word with you. On those two counts you're wrong."

"Where am I right?"

71

"I can't be sure of that."

"Then where do you judge I'm right?"

"In thinking he guessed you're planning a scheme in the hills." Thompson paused to inhale smoke. "In some ways," he said, "Major Craig is a very odd man. A very odd man indeed."

"Is he?"

"*I* think so."

Ramsay stayed silent.

Thompson said, "We've been to the hills."

"You and Major Craig?"

"And Mrs Craig."

"When?"

"Some time ago. During the course."

"Why did you go, Staff?"

"To recce an area for the field training fortnight."

"Then he means to go there anyway?"

Thompson put his hand out very slowly, and tapped the ash from his cigarette. "I wouldn't have said that, Mr Ramsay. I thought the recce was a great success. The area's ideal for what you have in mind."

"Didn't Major Craig agree with you?"

"I don't know, Mr Ramsay. When we got back I thought it was all buttoned up. Then he dropped this bombshell."

"What bombshell?"

"About making the scheme a cadet competition. At first I thought he meant a competition for a scheme set in the hills. But he didn't. He never gave the hills as a term of reference. And when I thought about it, how could he, Mr Ramsay? None of you chaps have been to the hills. I reckon some of you don't even realize they're there. It was interesting when the schemes started to come in. The majority of them weren't planned for a particular area, but they weren't the sort of schemes that would work in the jungle. Like you said, Mr Ramsay, they were all static, all full of set-piece battles. The sort that you drafted and threw away."

"Staff, may I ask a question?"

"Go ahead."

"Why do you think Major Craig guesses I want a scheme set in the hills?"

"I'm not talking to you as a cadet? I'm talking to you man to man?"

Ramsay nodded.

Thompson said, "I could crawl out from under that one simply by saying that all I meant was that you mentioned the Chota Bandar to Mrs Craig, Major Craig heard you, and put two and two together. But that wouldn't convince you, would it?"

"Not really, Staff."

"So I'll tell you. There are three men in this Company who know where the scheme *ought* to be. Me, you, and the Company Commander. And each of us knows that the other two know."

"Why do you include me?"

Thompson looked at him steadily. "I'm disappointed, Ramsay. I didn't expect you to question that."

Ramsay hesitated. "I was interested in *your* reasons for including me."

"Vanity then, Mr Ramsay, and not false modesty?"

Ramsay said, "Yes, all right, vanity."

"You're good. You're bloody good. You've got the proper soldiering instinct. It stands out a mile. The others are beginning to dislike you and that's always a good sign. Perhaps dislike isn't the right word. You make them feel uncomfortable. A chap who's a bit different, a bit better, a bit brainier, a chap who's got a vocation for something always makes others feel uncomfortable. That's what's happening to you. I've watched it happening almost right from the beginning."

Thompson put his head on one side. "You have it in you to be a bigger bastard than I could ever be. You have it in you to be a soldier streets ahead of me. There could come a time, Mr Ramsay, when I'd hate your guts. I'm not joking. I'm an old soldier. I've seen it happen."

Ramsay smiled and said, "Shouldn't a good officer inspire affection?" The word came out shapeless.

"What are you asking me to say, Mr Ramsay? What you already know?"

73

"What do I already know?"

"That an officer should only inspire confidence. There's a sort of warped affection wrapped up in it. Not their sort of affection. Our sort of affection. But I don't like the word. Affection for a man won't save his bacon."

Ramsay said, "I've got another question, Staff. If Major Craig knows that the scheme should be in the jungle, why does he hang back?"

"They say he had a bad time walking out of Burma."

"You think he's afraid of the jungle?"

"Afraid's not a good word to use about a soldier."

"But that's what you mean, Staff."

Thompson inhaled more smoke. "Yes, Mr Ramsay. That's what I mean."

Ramsay moved his head so that once more he stared at the blank piece of paper. He heard Thompson say, "I think both of us had better try and forget what I've just said," and then he was weary of him. The room was too full of Thompson and the paper was still blank.

"Yes, Staff," he said. He looked up. "How can I get to the Chota Banda—?" he asked.

"I'll take you."

"Thank you, Staff. When?"

"During the week's break, when we're off duty next week. I'll get a truck from the MT Sergeant. He's a pal of mine."

"Will Major Craig approve?"

"The idea, frankly, Mr Ramsay, is that Major Craig won't know about the truck. It wouldn't do for me to be helping you in the competition."

"He'll think I've gone by bus?"

"Yes."

"Then oughtn't I to go by bus, Staff?"

"Mrs Craig overlooked the fact that native transport is out of bounds. It's doubtful you'd be let on."

"Then the alternative is by bicycle or on foot."

"Thirty miles each way, Mr Ramsay. With temperatures in the nineties. It would take you three or four days and the sleeping would be rough."

Ramsay smiled. "The Chota Bandar is virtually unattainable, isn't it?"

"That is the general idea."

"Would I be allowed to go on foot?"

"No, Mr Ramsay. You would need a pass and we shouldn't issue one. Cadets aren't encouraged to wander around outside the cantonment."

"But how should I explain to Major Craig how I'd recced the area for the scheme I produced?"

Thompson looked at his fingernails. "I imagine you would say you scrounged a ride in transport going that way."

"It would sound pretty thin."

"Are you worried about it sounding pretty thin?"

"No, Staff."

"If you think about it you'll see that if there's some sort of mystery about how you got there then, providing you haven't been caught out of bounds, Craig'll think you've *been* out of bounds and got away with it."

"Out of bounds meaning by native bus or hitch-hiking?"

"Exactly. It'd be a feather in your cap—unofficially. He might even think you'd walked. It's easy to leave the school by the south road and nobody would be missed in mess during the holiday."

Ramsay nodded. He watched Thompson and wondered about his motives.

Thompson got up, "Well, shall I lay it on?"

Ramsay stood. "Yes."

"I suggest the Wednesday. OK?"

"OK."

"I'll drop in Tuesday evening when I'm sure about the transport."

"Right you are, Staff."

At that moment he came to his decision. As they reached the door he said, "Could I have a map meanwhile? I'd like to get the feel of the place."

"Drop in to Company office tomorrow about 1700 hours. I'll give you one then. Good night, Mr Ramsay."

"Good night, Staff."

Thompson went. Ramsay shut the door and came back into the empty room, to the sheaf of blank white paper.

He set out on the Tuesday morning several hours before it was light. He went on foot, dressed in khaki drill trousers, ammunition boots, while civilian shirt and topee. He carried a pack in which Abdul had put emergency rations of chocolate and tinned meat, and a water-bottle. Around the pack was strapped a blanket. Tucked in the rear pocket of his trousers was the map which Thompson had lent him.

He thought of Craig and of Thompson, and of John and of the thing Craig was waiting for him to find. He did not believe, as Thompson did, that Craig was afraid of the jungle. If Craig were afraid of the jungle he would not so have left things that any man, a man like Ramsay himself, could choose the jungle. He would have had done with it; himself choosing the plain he would have had done with it. But he had not chosen the plain. He had chosen nothing. He had waited for Ramsay to choose. He had known what Ramsay would choose. In this way did not Craig choose the same thing? Was not this journey to the hills a journey Craig expected him to make, a journey Craig wanted him to make?

Was it not Craig's journey as much as his own?

Ramsay (5)

HE RESTED from the heat of Tuesday, twelve miles from the school, in the dark interior of a ruined temple. He had not seen the temple from the road; only the copse which sheltered it. Old goat droppings crusted the floor and from the road below the hill he heard, through sleep, the creak of bullock carts and the gentle, high-pitched tinkle of their bells.

At evening he woke and knew peace. He walked to the village in the fading light. Dogs and children greeted him. The air was spiced. Dung fires cooked meals and young women bathed in the pool. He was brought to the headman's family and begged water and chappatties of them. They wondered, but gave him water and the unleavened wheaten pancakes warm from the fire, brought him rice and curried vegetable; surrounded him with their suspicion and their friendliness and their silence.

He walked on through the darkness, his hearing and sense of smell sharpened by it, so that these senses illuminated and gave dimensions to it. Lawson had said: You don't notice people, you only notice things. Lawson had meant to say: You notice things more than you do people, but had said it the other way round to give it greater impact. As Ramsay became accustomed to the darkness he became excited. He was alone on the road which led to the hills. The hills would unfold themselves for him at last and prove the logic of his longing for them.

He marched steadily at four miles an hour, rested each hour for ten minutes. Towards midnight the jackals began their crying, sometimes near by, sometimes far off. The land became wider and the night emptier.

He entered the forest at first light, climbed to the crest of the northern ridge and lay down to sleep. He had come to an area where trees had fallen and the forest lay partially open to the sky. Whenever he opened his eyes he could see the last stars.

He rose, retreated into the forest, lay down where the sky above was scarcely visible and the coming daylight would less disturb his rest, closed his eyes again. He pulled the blanket over his head to protect it from the mosquitoes.

When he woke he found that the blanket had fallen away from his face and that the sun shone into the clearing a few yards away. He opened his pack, which he had used as a pillow, drank some water, and ate one of the chappatties he had saved from the previous evening. His eyes were gummed, the tips of his fingers and toes numb, the skin tight over his cheekbones. There was stubble on his chin.

Leaving his pack and blanket he walked to the clearing. Where it was in shadow the grass was heavily dewed. He stripped off his shirt, meaning to rub his face and arms and chest with his moistened hands, and then, on impulse, removed the rest of his clothing and stood there naked for a moment. Then he lay down and rolled over in the wet grass. Sharp twigs and stones, buried in the grass, tore at his skin. He stood again and in the sunlight massaged his arms and legs. Life surged through him. With the sudden arrogance of wellbeing he wished to go naked through the forest so that his soft skin would toughen and coarsen; live in the forest naked, savagely, until his whiteness had gone and his muscles had bunched and hardened.

He let the warmth of the sun dry him as he sat, still naked, on the branch of a fallen tree. He looked at the tree. It was dead. He was alive. He rose, dressed himself. He went back into the forest, rolled up his blanket and bound it to the pack. It was ten o'clock by his watch. He drew out the map and glanced at it briefly. He knew it by heart. He would go down the slope to the road and then climb to the crest of the centre ridge and down again to the river. It was the river he had come to see. With any luck he could be there by midday. Humping the pack, he set off.

As he came out of the forest to the road which separated the northern and centre ridges he saw the truck.

For a minute or so he stayed on the fringe of the trees and studied it. It was an Army truck, an 8-cwt utility van. It was parked on the roadside about one hundred yards away. He narrowed his eyes and made out, against the glare, the sign-plate on the tailboard. The truck had come from the school.

Ahead, the road ran straight for a mile or so until it was lost in the converging spurs that prickled from the sides of the northern and centre ridges. There was no one on the road.

He began to quarter the ground, the spurs of the centre ridge, sparsely covered with forest; the ground on the slope of the centre ridge immediately to the right of the truck. This ground was levelled by wood-cutters. He watched this ground intently. The truck was drawn up there deliberately. Someone had left the truck and walked across the denuded ground to reach the lower fringes of forest on the centre ridge.

He moved cautiously into the road. From where he now stood he could see right through the open back of the truck to the windscreen. No one sat at the wheel. He crossed to the other side of the road and went into the jungle. He climbed the slope, skirting the clearing, paused every minute or so to listen. He was grateful to the forest, for it hid him from the eyes of the man he tracked.

He had decided that it was only one man. It was Thompson. He trudged on up the steepening slope. The clearing to his left gave way to jungle and now Ramsay paused more often. As the jungle darkened he grew conscious of the whiteness of his shirt. Quickly he put down his pack, removed the shirt and stuffed it inside a fold of the blanket. He gathered earth in his hands, spat on it and rubbed it on his arms, chest and face. It was makeshift camouflage, but it would have to do. After he had replaced the pack on his shoulders he cut off some foliage and laced it into the band of his topee, and into the belt of his trousers, so that the fronds of leaf and fern grew up around his nakedness, disrupted its recognizable outlines.

He reached the top of the ridge and halted there, rested the weight of his pack against the trunk of a tree.

There was something wrong, some sense in which he felt incomplete. He put a hand in his trouser pocket and closed his fingers over the jack-knife which was secured by a cord to a button at his waist. He pulled the knife out, hefted it without looking at it, but as he hefted it he knew what was wrong and why he felt incomplete. Apart from the knife he had no arms.

He looked at the knife, snapped the blade open and tested its edge with the ball of his thumb. Blunt. Useless. He smiled and asked himself, 'What do you want with arms? There's no enemy.' A twig snapped. Ramsay froze, the knife gripped in his hand, his thumb raised above the blade. The knife was pointed outward in the direction of the sound. The knife was an extension of his tensed arm. He folded his thumb over the fingers which gripped the handle.

The sound was not repeated, but Ramsay did not relax. Someone had trodden on a twig and the twig had snapped.

Now that someone had moved away. There was an enemy. Another man in the forest was potentially an enemy. Ramsay stayed quite still. The sound of the breaking twig had come from a place directly ahead. If the man had been coming forward he would be visible now, amongst the trees. He had gone either to the left or the right or straight on, away from Ramsay.

Ramsay waited. Again his stomach knotted with that odd excitement. The blood had come to his head and pulsed there. The whole of his body seemed to prickle.

He could not be sure, afterwards, whether he had heard some small sound of movement down to his right. When he thought about it, at other times, it seemed as though that is what must have happened. But then, standing alone and waiting for some sign, he suffered a muffling of senses on the left side of his body and a sharpening of those on the right so that he turned in that direction and went cautiously down the slope. And now both to the right and the left he experienced that curious muffling of sound, a muffling on either side of a channel of clarity which led him with certainty forward in the direction of the river. So strange was this sensation that at first he was afraid, but when it persisted he understood its purpose and then he was not afraid but excited in a new way; excited not at the intimation of power, but with the power itself as he felt it clothe him in invulnerability.

All at once the muffling went and the forest was alive on all sides of him and so he stood stock still. In the distance he heard the screech of monkeys. He moved forward cautiously, changed his mind and knelt suddenly. There was a track ahead and a man was coming back along it.

The man was walking slowly, picking his way across the ground. He stopped a few feet away from Ramsay, but did not look in Ramsay's direction. Ramsay saw that the other man did not sense his presence. The other man was Craig.

Craig took out a packet of cigarettes, lit one, and sat down. Once he looked sharply towards where Ramsay was hidden, but seemed then to be reassured that he was alone. When he had finished his cigarette he got to his feet and went back up the hill.

Five minutes later Craig's voice rang through the forest. He called Ramsay's name. He called Ramsay's name three times, and Ramsay could tell that each time Craig shouted he faced in a different direction.

Ramsay stood up, threw away the camouflage foliage, put on his shirt and followed Craig up the hill. While he climbed he wondered at the mistake he had made in believing the man in the forest had been Thompson. He should have known it was Craig. Thompson had discovered his absence, reported it to Craig, hinted at his whereabouts. And Craig had come to find him, to watch him. But Craig had failed in that. The boot had been on the other foot. In the forest Craig had been blind, deaf. Ramsay paused. Like the herd, he thought, unable to see, unable to hear, needing to be led. Frustration jarred him. Was that all Craig had waited for, watched for? Proof that in the forest he, Ramsay, would still be a leader? A new thought came: Had John been the real leader too? Had Craig been useless to him in the jungle?

When he came to the edge of the forest he saw Craig approaching the truck beyond the clearing. He cupped his hands to his mouth and hollered.

Craig stopped and turned. It was like seeing him in slow motion. Ramsay stepped out of the forest and went down the slope to meet him, but Craig stayed by the truck.

As he drew nearer he noticed how old Craig looked; old, tired, past it, much older than John would have been if John had lived and not died in the jungle.

The sun beat down on him. There was an inescapable burden of heat, of heat and, unexpectedly, contempt.

Craig (5)

CRAIG SAW the stains on Ramsay's face and chest where his shirt was pulled open by the weight of his shoulder-pack and knew that these stains had been made with earth. A few stray leaves, clinging to Ramsay's topee, completed the picture.

Craig guessed that Ramsay had been close to him in the forest.

"Then it is you, Ramsay," he said.

"Yes, sir."

"Cut out the 'sir' while we're here."

"Right."

"Let's go in the shade. No, not in the truck. It's like an oven in there. Under that tree."

They moved to the tree under which, a few weeks before, he had picnicked with Esther and Thompson. He sat down while Ramsay eased the pack off his back. When Ramsay had settled Craig said, "You know I was looking for you?"

"Yes, I heard you call."

"I'd better tell you how I guessed you were here, hadn't I?"

"Sergeant-Major Thompson suggested it, I suppose."

"Now, why do you say that?"

"I asked him for a map of the area and said I was planning a scheme here. If my absence has been discovered I suppose he put two and two together."

Craig nodded. He wondered whether to delve more deeply. He was a bit suspicious of Thompson, whose theories about Ramsay's absence were too pat, too closely matched now by Ramsay's own explanation. He decided that it was not important. He said, "Yes, that's how it was, Ramsay."

"How did he discover my absence?"

"I haven't said it was he who discovered it. Actually it was, which is probably fortunate for you. He's said nothing to anyone but me. Apparently he wanted to get the map back. Your servant eventually admitted you'd been gone nearly twenty-four hours. That was late last night. Thompson wanted to come with me today, but I thought it better if I came alone. You realize you've done a damn silly thing, Ramsay, something that could get you kicked out of the school?"

"Yes, I realize that."

"Did you walk all the way?"

"Yes."

"Have you eaten properly?"

"Yes, I've been all right."

"I shall take you back in the truck. We'll time our arrival for after dark and I shall drop you some way from your quarters so that you won't be seen being brought back by me."

"Thank you."

"I've got some food in the truck. Have you got any first-aid kit?"

"A bit. Why?"

"I thought you would have. I brought some all the same. I didn't expect to find you in any trouble, but it was best to be sure."

Ramsay said, "What sort of trouble?"

"A fall. Sprained ankle. Broken leg. A cut. Snake bite. There *are* snakes. Where have you slept?"

"In a temple yesterday. In the forest this morning. I marched by night because it was cooler."

Craig nodded. Ramsay had not asked what would happen to him for going out of bounds. He knew that nothing would happen. Craig considered the possibility of ending it for Ramsay by taking him back here, now, and charging him with absence without leave; of taking him in front of Manville—that dry, dead man. But he would not end it for Ramsay. It was not written that he should end it for Ramsay. It was only written that he should help Ramsay to find his own end in his own way.

After they had eaten lunch and rested they set off for the river. They did not speak as they went through the forest and although Craig led at first he gradually eased his pace and then deliberately dropped behind and followed in Ramsay's footsteps. When they reached the track which went in either direction to the river Ramsay didn't pause but turned, as if by instinct or from prior knowledge, to the right.

"The other way, Ramsay."

Ramsay turned round, but stuck his ground. He said after a moment, "It goes either way."

"How do you know?"

"I think the map says so."

"The map may be wrong. They often are."

"I don't think it's wrong here. The river bends right round.

If we cut straight ahead through the jungle we should come out at the top of the spur, where the river bends."

"Did you get as far as this this morning?"

"No."

"Then what besides the map tells you that either way would do?" He watched Ramsay closely. The flat look had come back. "Instinct?" he prompted.

The boy became even more guarded.

"Don't scoff at instinct, Ramsay. Your brother had it. Jungle instinct. The ability to feel the ground ahead of you—poke your head metaphorically above the trees and get the whole lie of the land, like being in an aeroplane, high up." Craig paused. The first actual turn of the screw was the most difficult. "If you've got it, it's like the forest talking to you," he said. He added, "It doesn't talk to me. At least, not in that way, but I think it talks to you. It talked to John." He paused again. "Now, Ramsay, which way?"

Ramsay hadn't taken his eyes off Craig. "We'll go the way you decide, sir."

Craig said, "No, Ramsay. The way you decide. And I asked you not call me 'sir' while we're here."

Without another word Ramsay swung back to take the track to the right and Craig followed him. Soon they came to the river.

The channel of water was narrower, but the pool below the ford had changed little.

"So you were right," Craig said. "The track leads to the river in both directions. What do you make of it now you're here?"

"Of the river?"

"Yes. What picture will it present in June?"

"It gets drier, I suppose, up until the monsoon."

"And then?"

"It's in spate."

"And this ford?"

"Virtually disappears."

"And below it?" Craig prompted.

"Where the channel widens?"

"Yes. What happens there?"

"It's a sort of basin, isn't it?"

Craig nodded. "That's what it looks like. Go and have a look at it."

Ramsay slithered down the bank and walked across the bed to the channel, followed the channel along to the point where it widened. The mud was sucking at his boots. Suddenly he bent down, undid his boots and took them off. He took off his socks and began to undress. Naked, he walked into the pool. Within a few feet he was out of his depth and had plunged in. He surfaced and then headed himself in again. Ripples spread.

Craig went down the bank and walked a little way into the river bed. His heart hammered. He counted the seconds, knew a moment's panic, lost thread of his counting. Then Ramsay's head and shoulders shot above the water at the other side of the pool. He took a deep breath and went under again. Again Craig counted. Ramsay was under for thirty seconds. He surfaced in the middle of the pool and breast-stroked to the edge. When he stood up his hands and feet were covered in mud. His right shin was bloody.

"It's a natural basin," he said. "About ten feet deep at this end. There's a sort of rocky ledge the other end."

"You've grazed your leg on it."

"I know. You could get wedged in it."

Ramsay gathered up his clothes and followed Craig to the bank. Craig sat on the bank whilst Ramsay stood in the river bed and let the sun dry him. The mud caked, he rubbed it off, and then dressed, leaving off his boots and socks. Later Craig removed his own boots and socks, rolled up his trousers and followed Ramsay over the ford to the other side.

Here the jungle was thicker, subtly different. There was a musty smell about it that was absent on the centre ridge. Farther up the hill they heard the sound of water gurgling over rock, followed the sound and came to a tumbling stream. They went back down the hill by the side of the stream and found the place at which it went underground. It was the answer to the pool in the river bed. The stream joined the river subterraneously.

"There must be an outlet into the basin, Ramsay. Lucky you didn't swim into it."

"I didn't find one."

"It must be there. But perhaps it's not big. Probably the ledge is part of it."

They returned to the river, dropped down into the bed and walked along its course, around the spur and so to the point where Elephant Hill revealed itself. Craig watched for the moment when Ramsay would see the hill. The moment came and Ramsay stood still.

"So that's what it looks like," he said. "I thought the contours of the map were odd."

"You didn't expect it to look like that on the ground?"

"I think I knew it ought to, but I didn't expect it to."

"Let's go in that direction, Ramsay." Craig looked at his watch. "We must turn back in half an hour."

They returned to the bank, climbed up and entered the jungle again. For fifteen minutes they slogged. Craig ordered a halt. He offered Ramsay a cigarette. They smoked in silence.

Then Ramsay said, "Was it a place like this?"

Craig, knowing, still asked, "Was what a place like this?"

"The place where John died."

He looked at Ramsay. "Yes, a place somewhat like this."

Ramsay looked straight back at him. "You haven't told me everything about it, have you?"

"Haven't I?"

"I don't think so. You were going to tell me that first night, but thought better of it."

"What was I going to tell you, Ramsay?"

"That when he asked you to finish him off, so that he shouldn't be a liability, you did finish him off."

Craig said, "I see."

He turned away from Ramsay. Now that Ramsay had said it he believed that he had expected him to say it.

"You did finish him off, didn't you?"

Craig sat very still. He felt the need to tell the truth. He did not understand why it was suddenly hard to tell. He said, "That's an interesting supposition. Say that for the moment I

86

don't answer it, but ask you instead what you would have done if you had been me?"

Ramsay was silent. Craig watched him, saw the deepening of Ramsay's eyes as the boy looked into himself, into his humanity, the mirror that endangered Craig's purpose; and then Craig knew, reluctantly, why he evaded the truth.

Ramsay said, "I think I would have finished him."

"Why?"

"I don't know. Because he was in pain and going to die anyway, I suppose." Ramsay paused. "Is that why you did it?"

Craig seized the straw. *Going to die anyway.* The mirror *was* cracked then. He said, "I haven't said that I did."

"No. But you did, didn't you?"

"I'd rather not say, Ramsay."

"There's no need. You don't need to say. I know now that you did."

Craig said, "There are things that we can never *know*. We guess at them." He stood up, looked down at Ramsay. "Come on. We'd better get going."

He started off down the hill and heard Ramsay following him. Ramsay got closer. Craig fought the desire to turn and face him, kept on, his back open to attack. Suddenly he felt his arm caught in a strong grip. He stumbled and Ramsay let go but stepped in front of him so that he had to stop.

"I want to know."

"Why do you want to know?"

"He was my brother. I've a right to know how he died. You can't leave it like that."

Craig snapped, "That's how I choose to leave it." He was only part uncertain. The other part of him trembled with excitement. The vein in Ramsay's neck stood out like a cord, a sign of anger. For the moment the anger was all, the reasons for it—distorted, muddled as they were—nothing. This was a new Ramsay. This Ramsay was partly his own creation.

"That's how I choose to leave it," Craig repeated. "We'll talk no more about it."

He brushed past Ramsay and left him to follow on.

Ramsay (6)

HE WATCHED Craig disappear into the jungle. For about a minute he could hear the diminishing noise of his progress. Distantly Craig's voice came, "Come on, Ramsay." Then slowly he went down the hill too.

Craig had killed John. Scrambling out of the river John had gone into the jungle and after a while the smell of death had come up from the ground. The sound of the river and of the rain and the smell of death were John's last possessions in the world: these, and pain.

Ramsay, coming to his own river and seeing that Craig must already have crossed, asked himself: What do I possess? He stared at the flowing water. John was in pain, and had said to Craig: Finish me off. As Ramsay thought the words he could hear John saying them. He had almost forgotten the quality, the actuality of John's voice, but he heard it again now. Finish me off. And Craig had finished him off.

Craig said: What would you have done in my place? Now Ramsay reformulated the question. He thought: If I had a gun and Craig said, Finish me off, what would I do?

He knelt down by the bank and took off his boots and socks. He walked over the river bed and into the shallow channel which scarcely came above his knees. On the opposite bank he rested for a moment before putting his boots and socks on again. The shadows in the river bed were lengthening.

It appeared to him now that when he left the river and entered the forest to join Craig, as he would, he would leave something behind him for ever. He did not know what it was. In a way it was connected with John, with all of the past. He wondered whether after all there was nothing in the forest that he could find, only something he would lose and that this was what Craig had waited for. He wanted Craig to come back and tell him, 'No, I didn't finish it for John.' But as he considered this he realized the implication it would carry that

John had died slowly, in agony, and that Craig had let him.

By the time he left the river bed the death of his brother had begun to assume an unimportance, and anger to give way to detachment. He could not answer the question: Should Craig have finished him off? And because he could not answer the question he no longer asked it.

PART TWO: THE RIVER

May to June, 1943

INFORMATION

The northern half of India has been occupied by the enemy. Our own forces occupy the southern half. For the purpose of the exercise the hills of the Chota Bandar will be considered as extensive and as forming a natural barrier between the forces. Our own forces avoided annihilation by escaping south through this jungle. It is thought that enemy activity in the jungle is confined only to routine patrol work south of the river in the dry season. The road between the north and centre ridge is one of the enemy's lines of communication, but is not protected in strength, according to air reconnaissance reports.

INTENTION

Our own forces will send a self-supporting penetration group into the Chota Bandar from the south to gather information about the enemy's dispositions in the region of the southern, centre and northern ridge, and to harry the enemy in those regions by any method open to them, disrupting where possible their lines of communication.

METHOD

(*a*) The penetration group will be called RAMFORCE.

(*b*) The enemy will be represented by a company of an Indian Infantry battalion drawn from a local training camp.

(*c*) RAMFORCE will be led by O/Cadet R. W. Ramsay and will consist of D Cadet Company, mounted as three columns of platoon strength under commanders to be appointed. Second-in-command of RAMFORCE will be O/Cadet Lawson.

(*d*) Mules, drawn from the school reserve, will provide column transportation. Mules will be in the charge of cadets under Supervision Indian Muleteer.

(*e*) RAMFORCE will proceed by route-march from the school to a forming-up area at a time and date to be fixed by Major Craig. For the purpose of the exercise the forming-up area will represent a halt in the approach march of the penetration group. The forming-up area and the line of approach to it will not be divulged in advance by the RAMFORCE Commander to any but the Chief Umpire.

(*f*) The Chief Umpire will be Major C. Craig. Assistant Umpires: Sergeant-Major Thompson and Staff Sergeant Shaw.

(*g*) Situations will be evolved and developed on the ground by the Commander of RAMFORCE and the Chief Umpire.

(*h*) The 'Enemy' will take up their dispositions on the fifth day of the exercise.

ADMINISTRATION

(*a*) Scale stores, rations and ammunition (blank) for RAMFORCE will be laid down by Major Craig in consultation with Comd RAMFORCE.

(*b*) RAMFORCE will be considered as capable of receiving supplies by airdrop.

INTERCOMMUNICATION

(*a*) Comd RAMFORCE will have at his disposal 30-cwt truck and water-wagon, drawn from school MT section, for transportation of stores from the school to the area of the exercise.

(*b*) Chief Umpire will have at his disposal 8-cwt utility truck for umpiring purposes and general administration outside the scope of the exercise.

Craig (1)

ON THE southern face of Elephant Hill there were. clearings as though man had once lived there. On the uppermost of these the foundations of a simple square building lay where three tracks intersected. For a man standing in this clearing the whole region of wooded hills which lay to the south of the three main ridges of the Chota Bandar was spread out below him.

Craig said to his companion, "Well, that's where we'll come from."

Lieutenant Blake lowered his binoculars and turned to Craig and Craig recognized the now familiar, half-amused, half-wary look which people gave him. Blake was a big man, dark, with a face battered almost into expressionlessness by a determination to do well. The mixture of amusement and wariness coordinated it briefly and disclosed weakness.

Blake said, "It's a lot of country, sir. Which way will you come in?"

"You aren't even supposed to know that we are coming."

Blake looked at his map. After a while he let it fall again to his side. His lips were compressed, dimpled slightly at the corners. He meant to convey that he had judged the proposed line of approach, but Craig knew that he hadn't. He would sit up late, drink too much beer, and, when he had reached a decision, be then uncertain about it.

"All right, Blake?"

"All right, sir."

"Let's make our way back then."

The river was dried to a trickle, but the basin gleamed wide and still. They crossed where he and Ramsay had crossed, but had no need to take off boots and socks. At the bank, Craig stopped.

"This," he said, gesturing at the river, "—this is the unknown quantity."

"Oh?" Blake puckered his brow.

"By the time we get here it might be in spate."

"Yes, of course."

They plodded along the track and up the slope of the centre ridge. When they got down to the road where their two trucks waited for them Blake said, "I'll get my chap to brew up if you've time for a cup."

"Thank you. I'd like that."

Craig sat beneath the trees and watched Blake convey their wishes to his driver and then in an excess of manly unconcern urinate openly at the roadside. He walked back to Craig buttoning his trousers.

"Where will you establish your headquarters?" Craig asked him.

"I thought up here."

Craig nodded.

Blake said, "You'll be coming round to look at us when we've got ourselves organized, sir?"

"I expect so."

"Just before your chaps put in their attack?"

Craig smiled. "Before. Not necessarily just before. If you knew it was just before, then as soon as I'd been you'd all be on the alert."

Blake grinned. "No harm in trying it on, sir," he said. "So far as I can see we might be sitting on our fannies for ten days or be rousted up a few hours after we've moved in. As it's only an exercise I thought it'd be nice to know how we stand."

Craig said, "It's more than an exercise."

"Meaning, sir?"

"Meaning only that. It's more than an exercise." He met Blake's stare. "Stop thinking of it as an exercise, Blake. You're a conqueror. Your armies have conquered all that." He waved his hand northwards. "You've cut through it like wire through cheese. Over there you've got the fleshpots, but down here you're just sweating it out. You've got a rifle company stuck out on a front line that's been as quiet as the grave for a year. This road links you to your front-line posts and connects you with your rear. Over the hill there's the river and then miles of jungle. You're told that if ever the enemy attacks you in any sort of strength it won't be in this part of the world. Anything big-scale will be on the plains far to the east or the west. All the same, you've got your section of hill and river and road to look after—much too big an area for the number of troops—so you send patrols out into the jungle beyond the river and you maintain a look-out from Elephant Hill. Boring, routine stuff. But real. Not an exercise. The real thing, Blake, the real thing."

Tea came, scalding hot, in two mugs.

"Sorry about the mugs, sir," Blake said.

"Why, do they leak?"

Blake flushed. "No. I don't think so. I meant sorry I've got no cups."

"Why should you? You're a soldier on active service. Or you will be tomorrow. What time do you expect to get your chaps here?"

"My orders say 1500 hours. I'll have 'em here by then." Blake sipped his tea, blew across the steaming surface between sips. "Was there any particular reason why we should only come in on the fifth day of the exercise?" He subtly emphasized the last word.

"Yes. It cuts down the period you have to wait around for something to happen and also gives Ramforce time to reach their forming-up area."

Blake glanced at him, grinned and said, "I suppose it's no good asking you where they're forming up, sir?"

"My answer is that they're forming up in what to you is enemy territory." Craig smiled back at him, suddenly liking him for his obstinacy. "It really *is* important that you shouldn't know where Ramforce is. You know they're coming here and they know you're here. That's the only gesture to unreality I have to make. You won't know which way they're coming and they won't know your actual dispositions or patrol routine, even if I shall. Thanks for the tea, Blake." He stood up. Blake just beat him to it, took his empty mug. Together they went to their trucks.

Craig said, "Don't let those sepoys of yours get the idea they're on holiday. As from 1500 hours tomorrow you're open to attack."

"Don't worry, sir. I'll keep 'em on their toes. They're good types."

"I'll say *au revoir* then, Blake."

They shook hands and Blake stood back and saluted.

Craig told his driver to take him back to the school. Every few minutes Craig looked over his shoulder. Blake's truck followed unostentatiously, much farther behind than was necessary to avoid the dust plume. The road wound out of the northern valley and, free of it, sent a narrower track off to the west. Six miles farther on another track branched out eastwards. Craig smiled to himself at the thought of Blake keeping pace to see which of the tracks he took.

After they had passed the intersection of the eastern track he told the driver to slow down and stop as if they had engine trouble. In a few moments Blake drew up in front of him.

"Can I help, sir?"

"Yes, I think you can. Take me back to the school, will you?"

"The school?"

"I've got some admin to lay on."

"What about your truck?"

"Oh, he'll put it right in a jiffy. But I'm in a hurry."

Blake grinned. "I'll leave my chap with him. They can sort it out together."

"That would be fine."

For a while Blake drove without speaking. Then he looked at Craig, back at the road ahead and said, "You beat me that time. I hoped to see you take the left track or the right track, so's I'd know better where your chaps were."

"You can rest assured, Blake, that whatever move I made would have been deceptive, and as I neither want to help you nor deceive you, I thought this was the best way. We see each other safely back to school. We wait for my truck, which has nothing wrong with it, and go our separate ways, but this time from neutral ground."

Blake laughed aloud. "Fair enough, sir," he said.

"Yes, I thought so."

"Are you going back to the jungle today?"

"After I've had tea in civilized surroundings. I tell you what, Blake. Come and have tea at my bungalow."

"Thank you very much, sir."

"We'll leave a message for my driver at Company office."

At the bungalow they found Esther with her hair in pins.

"Now you've caught me," she said.

"This is the enemy commander, Mr Blake."

"I'm pleased to meet you, Mrs Craig."

"And I'm pleased to meet you, curlers or no curlers. I hate it when Colin's away. This damned bungalow isn't home to us yet."

But Craig thought: Yes, it is home. Where Esther is is home.

He caught her hand. She smiled, returned pressure.

"How's Ramsay doing?"

"Giving us hell."

"You look well on it."

"Do I?" He felt pleasure. "But I've not foot-slogged like the rest of them. Chief umpire is a sinecure."

Hussein brought tea, fussed over Craig.

"Hussein wanted to join you, Colin," Esther said. To Blake she added, "We've had him since we were married."

Blake said, youthfully wise, "He's a Pathan, isn't he?"

"He pretends to be."

"He could be a tough customer though, I should think."

Esther laughed. "But Hussein wouldn't hurt a fly."

Exaggeration. Craig leaned back. Esther exaggerated to make conversation.

"Well, I don't know," Blake said. "Some of the fellows in my company give that impression. Rouse 'em and you know different."

Craig watched them. There was a warmth in Esther which put younger men immediately at ease because they partly misinterpreted it. Blake was misinterpreting it now. Craig could see the way in which a man turned on his sex-appeal by watching Esther's face. He could tell what she was thinking. To know what Esther thought of a man gave his own estimate of him a greater depth. He closed his eyes. A lot could be judged from voice alone. He wondered how many scores of men there had been in the past ten years on whom he had reserved final judgment until they had passed through the searching fire which Esther kindled.

The truck arrived, redirected from his company office.

"I'll have a bath before I go back," Craig said, and Blake, already on his feet, took his cue. "I'd better get back to camp. Thanks a lot for the tea, Mrs Craig."

After his bath Craig asked her, "Well, what d'you make of the enemy?"

The curlers were out of her hair. She sat brushing it, dressing-gowned, in front of the mirror. "Oh, he's a nice enough boy." Which meant, Craig knew, that she had seen no signs of soldierly qualities other than those which circumstance might produce in any man.

Hussein helped him into clean uniform.

"Is it going well, Colin?"

"We've not really started."

"How are the boys taking it?"

"Enjoying it so far, I believe."

"I thought you said Ramsay was giving them hell."

"He is."

"In what way?"

"He's force-marched them fifteen miles a day. In the heat."

"Fifteen miles isn't very much."

"Force-marched. Not route-marched."

"Four days at fifteen miles means sixty miles. Where on earth's he got them to?"

"Place called Nanyaganj. It's only thirty miles away. He took them a roundabout route."

"Is that the forming-up area?"

"Yes. It's a village about fifteen miles downstream of Elephant Hill. There's a bridge there."

"Is the river dry?"

"As a bone. Bit of wet marrow in the channel."

"So now he marches fifteen miles back to Elephant Hill through the jungle, is that it?"

"That's what we're going to discuss tonight."

"And the boys like it, hell and all?"

"I think so."

97

"Is he playing any little tricks?"

Craig looked up at her. "Why do you say that?"

She brushed her hair with slow rhythmic strokes. "Because he's like John and John used to. Surely you haven't forgotten?"

"I had. You mean like the private punishments not in the book?"

"And the exercise where he pretended some of the NCOs had live instead of blank, to teach them to keep their heads down."

"I'd forgotten that."

"What little tricks has young Ramsay played?"

"It wasn't a trick. An extra discipline, you could call it."

"Over what?"

"Water."

"Tell me."

"It was the day before yesterday."

"The second day."

"That's it. He told them no water was to be drunk during the day because the water truck might not come in the evening. Most of them thought it was a joke."

"And it wasn't?"

"Partly. The water truck rendezvoused. Most of the chaps' bottles were empty. He let the cookhouse draw water then sounded an air-raid alarm. At the end of the raid he said the water truck had been destroyed. He sent it back almost full."

"And they liked that?"

"They didn't like it. They saw the point. And he had warned them."

"Had you sanctioned it, Colin?"

"Yes."

"Specifically?"

"How do you mean?"

"Specifically sanctioned the destruction of the water truck?"

"I'd specifically sanctioned the creation of fictional situations which might involve actual hardship. It's the point of the exercise."

"Had you visualized hardship about water?"

Craig saw that she watched him in the mirror.

"I visualize any hardship. Any hardship. Why do you disapprove in the case of water?"

"I don't disapprove."

"You disapprove of young Ramsay."

Another woman, Craig anticipated, would say: Do I? Esther shrugged. "Don't ask me why. My disapproval must be entirely unreasonable. As unreasonable as the boys' thirst would appear to them. Real, but no real fault of his." She swung round on the stool. She smiled. "I'd give anything to be with you."

"A film director would find a way." He had risen. He leant over her and kissed her hair. She grasped his arm and held it tightly for a moment.

"Now I shall have to go."

"Yes." She said, "Shall I see you again before the scheme's over?"

"A chief umpire is pretty mobile. But I don't promise anything."

"That means I won't."

She came with him to the door. The sun was setting.

He said, "Do you know what it is tomorrow?"

"No, Colin."

"A year since John Ramsay died."

"Is it?" she replied. He felt in her a curious withdrawal.

On the way back to Nanyaganj he thought about it. He wondered how much Esther had disliked the elder Ramsay. He could not recall at this distance what knowledge of Ramsay he had gained through Esther, but the more he thought about it the clearer became the picture of Ramsay as a man about whom Esther had taught him nothing. Whatever I knew of Ramsay, he told himself, I learned for myself.

They approached the track that went eastward to cut into the Chota Bandar where the eastern spurs levelled into the plain.

"Turn off here," he told the driver. The driver obeyed. It was partly along this track that the younger Ramsay had force-marched the Company. For the duration of the exercise the supply trucks from the school would take this route and be unobserved by Blake and his men astride the main road below the northern ridge. The driver switched both headlights on. The track was in bad condition. Craig hung on, became mesmerized by the road sliding towards them within the arc of light. He thought: I shall sleep. But he was still awake when they joined up again with the main road some fifteen miles east of the place where he and Blake had begun the drive home that afternoon. They followed the road east for half a mile, slowed down for the light bridge across the dry river, then drove steadily and slightly uphill for a mile to the village of Nanyaganj. The village slept. Only a long black dog, its eyes momentarily inflamed by the glare, contested their approach. Beyond the village the light of a cadet fire painted the shapes of trees on to the darkness.

They resumed their singing after he had said good night. He climbed up the slope of the hill to the patch of trees where a light shone dimly through the canvas of Ramsay's tent.

"May I come in, Ramsay?"

He had to stoop to enter through the flap which Ramsay, still seated, pushed aside. He could not stand upright and so sat immediately on the folding stool kept there for him. Ramsay had a similar stool. He had twisted round to face Craig, on it one elbow supported on the wooden crate on which a map was spread. The tent was very small. Only Craig and Thompson were similarly housed, farther down the hill. The rest in shelters constructed of branches.

Craig said, "Well, I've met the enemy. They'll be in position as from 1500 hours tomorrow. They're going in by lorry."

"Good."

"OC tried to pump me about where you were now and your line of approach. I expect he hopes to hold you up with strong patrol attacks."

"He'd need to send them in the right direction."

"Exactly."

Slowly Ramsay removed from his pocket a crumpled packet of cigarettes. Craig watched him. Ramsay had become noticeably slower, noticeably deliberate in all his physical movements. It was his eyes which fascinated Craig. The flatness was still there, but it was a flatness which might express a profound excitement, a fever disguised, undiagnosed, unchecked.

As Craig took the offered cigarette Ramsay said, "Did he see which direction you came from when you met on the road, sir?"

"No. I made a point of being there an hour before schedule."

"What about the way your truck was parked?"

"I took it off the road and parked it square."

"And coming away?"

"I took him back to the school and Esther gave him tea."

Ramsay looked down at the map.

Craig said, "I think you can count on his not knowing whether we're east or west or due south of him. Which is as it should be."

Ramsay nodded.

Craig smiled. "Well, now—this is where we begin in earnest. Let me expound my first situation. You've brought Ramforce to within fifteen miles of one of the enemy's positions on a thinly held line. So far you've moved through what we might call secondary jungle, but now you're faced with thick forest. Nanyaganj has been approached cautiously, but the inhabitants prove not only friendly but delighted to see the British again. From them you learn that only twice in the twelve months of enemy occupation have they been bothered by Jap patrols, who raided them for food. As the monsoon is due they don't expect to see them again until it's over. The bridge below the village is down and has never been repaired since the British blew it on the way out. The villagers prefer it that way."

Craig paused. Ramsay still looked at the map.

"They tell you that after the last monsoon the Japs established an outpost on the southern slope of a hill on this side of the river. You show them the map. The headman after a bit of help from you puts his finger on Elephant Hill. He offers to send a man into the hills to see if the outpost is still there or whether it's been abandoned and the men withdrawn by the parent company which he thinks has its headquarters on the northern ridge, commanding the road that eventually leads here to the bridge.

"I am a senior staff officer who has come to see how the independent penetration group is doing. You tell me all this and I ask you what you propose to do."

Ramsay looked at him and said, "I'm sorry, sir, but that's all a bit premature."

"Explain what you mean by premature."

"You're inferring that this is our forming-up point for the exercise."

"Isn't it?"

Ramsay turned to the map again. "I want to go farther south."

"You said Nanyaganj was to be the forming-up point."

"No, sir. You must have misunderstood me."

"I must have done. At the beginning of the series of forced-marches we agreed that we were making for Nanyaganj, Ramsay."

"I know. But I don't think I ever referred to it as the forming-up point."

In his right hand Ramsay held a pencil. Craig watched the point of the pencil which moved round in expanding circular forms and traced on the surface of the wooden crate a pattern of map contours.

Craig said, "How much farther south?"

"About twenty-five miles south-west."

"And where will that bring us to?"

"To a point fifteen miles due south of Elephant Hill."

"Let me look."

Ramsay gave him the map. For a few seconds Craig stared at it blindly. Meaningless.

"Where I've marked with a ring," Ramsay prompted.

Craig had to turn the map to read the name.

Khudabad.

The Place of God.

Ramsay spoke the name. "Khudabad."

"How do you propose to get there, Ramsay?"

"The road from Nanyaganj takes us there."

Craig looked for the road on the map. Ramsay was right. The thin black line, the dust road, snaked round the eastern face of the Chota Bandar, turned west and hugged the southern contours. At Khudabad, which as Ramsay had said was fifteen miles due south of Elephant Hill, the road swept on south across the plain.

"There's another interesting thing," Ramsay said.

"What?"

"The track that goes from Khudabad round the western slopes. The Chota Bandar is ringed completely by road."

"On the map, yes. On the ground it may have disappeared."

"I don't think so. The road that goes round the west of the hills eventually joins the main road back to the school."

"That's the track that goes off to the left when you're coming *away* from the northern valley."

"It crosses the river about five miles west of Elephant Hill."

"It's not marked as a bridge."

"It's a ford."

Craig said, "Where does all this get us, Ramsay?"

"Only to Khudabad."

"Will *that* be the forming-up point of the exercise?"

"We'll move into the jungle from there, yes."

"In which direction?"

"I'd prefer to decide at the time." Ramsay hesitated. "At Khudabad the inhabitants may tell me something."

"What's your programme for reaching Khudabad?"

"It's twenty-five miles. Two days' route-march."

"Not force-march?"

"No. We're within schedule. We can relax the atmosphere of urgency."

"I'm not so sure, Ramsay. You've spent four days getting to Nanyaganj. You'll spend another two getting to Khudabad. You'll probably spend one day resting *in* Khudabad——"

"Yes, I'll want an airdrop there."

"That's seven days. If you slog the fifteen miles to the Elephant Hill area straight you'll be going across the grain of the hills, switchback. In the jungle you won't average more than five miles a day. That's three days. If you take a detour you'll still need three days or more. Three on seven makes a total of ten. Blake's CO isn't going to be very pleased if the company he's lent us has to sit on its backside for five days."

"Who's Blake?"

"The chap who's commanding the enemy."

"I didn't know there was a limit."

"To what?"

"To the time the enemy's prepared to sit in the hills. I thought we had them for the duration of the scheme."

Craig handed back the map. He said, "We have. But they were made available on the tacit understanding that they'd get training in jungle warfare."

"They will."

"After five days doing nothing."

Ramsay passed a hand over his forehead. Beneath the smoothing fingers his eyebrows were raised, his eyelids lowered. He said, "They'll be patrolling."

"They might get tired of that after two or three days without bumping our chaps."

The eyelids flickered up.

"Yes, exactly, tired of patrolling."

Suddenly Craig understood. He felt defeated by Ramsay. He smiled, tried to put into his smile a hint of complicity.

"I know, Ramsay," he said, "but I'm not sure we'll be making the best use of them if we sap their alertness. Isn't that a factor to consider?"

"I don't think so."

Now Ramsay wasn't looking at him. Increasingly in Craig was this sense of Ramsay's withdrawal.

Ramsay said, "Above everything I want to establish reality."

"Yes. Reality." Craig heard the emptiness of his own voice. His mind wandered to Blake. He heard himself say to Blake: Not an exercise. The real thing, Blake, the real thing.

He said to Ramsay, "I agree."

"The enemy has been unmolested for a year. They think and act like——"

Craig supplied the word. "Conquerors."

"They lost their alertness months ago."

"Perhaps," Craig smiled. "There are other considerations."

"Such as?"

"Blake and his men might be new to the line. Fresh troops."

Ramsay said, "The chaps they took over from would tell

them it was easy. A sinecure. The outpost on Elephant Hill a bloody rest cure."

It was the first time Craig had heard Ramsay swear.

"What about intelligence, fifth columnists, Ramsay? Do you go on the assumption that your expedition is so secret?"

"No."

"Well, then."

"Partly no. Let's say there's a rumour about a penetration group somewhere in the forest."

"It would put them on the alert."

"At first. Not quite alert in that sense. It would give them the fidgets. When nothing happened they'd revert to boredom. The alert isn't the reality. Boredom or the fidgets are. That's what I'm after."

Craig thought back. All he could muster was, "You know nothing about an outpost on Elephant Hill yet. You told me the situation I developed was premature."

"Yes. But I may learn of it at Khudabad. My map tells me it's the highest ground. It doesn't tell me whether it gives visual command of the forest. It may be thick jungle up to its crest. But the map tells me to treat it with suspicion."

"Must we go to Khudabad, Ramsay?"

After a while Ramsay said, "Yes, sir."

"Then tell me the form as you visualize it."

Ramsay (1)

AFTER CRAIG had gone Ramsay lit a cigarette, opened his notebook and began to calculate. The camp was quiet. A cadet on the perimeter guard coughed. At midnight Ramsay rose stiffly, ducked and came out of the tent. He looked up at the night sky. They said that often it was at night that the clouds first gathered, low on the horizon, their shape illuminated by sheet lightning. But the sky was black, the stars needle-sharp. He picked his way to Lawson's bivouac.

"You're not asleep, then."

Lawson's cigarette end glowed as he inhaled before replying. "As you see."

"There's a change of plan."

"I'll be with you."

Alone, Ramsay returned to his tent, waited for Lawson.

Lawson came. The glow from the oil-lamp darkened the yellow of his jaundiced face. Ramsay stared at him.

"You ought to be in hospital."

"Sure."

"Do you want to go back?"

"Why? Stick it. That's what we're here for. To stick it. So I'll —— well stick it. Tell me the worst."

Ramsay referred to his notes, glanced back at Lawson.

"You'd better take it down."

"I'll remember."

"Can I bank on that?"

"Yes."

"You forgot to bring a notebook. You might forget something I tell you."

Lawson got up and left the tent. When he came back his notebook was open at the page, ready. "Shoot."

"Reveille 0400 hours. Tell the guard commander on your way back."

"Right."

"Parker's guard commander, isn't he?"

"Yes."

"Make sure he takes it in."

"I'll check him at 0345."

Their eyes met. Ramsay said, "Aren't you sleeping?"

"I get the squitters pretty regularly."

Ramsay put down his pencil; almost it dropped from his hand. He thought: A hint of exasperation, it's not what I mean to convey.

He said, "Look, you'd better go sick."

Lawson grinned. "Sod you, Bob. I wouldn't miss it for the world."

"Miss what?"

"The last round. Come on. Reveille 0400. What next?"

"What do you mean, the last round?"

Lawson said, "I meant the last round of the battle."

"Which battle?"

"Between you and Craig."

"I'm not aware of a battle."

"No. Well—come on. Let's get on with the orders."

"We have differences of opinion."

"Sure."

"We also agree about things every so often."

"No, you don't agree. You give in to each other from time to time. Or anyway, give the appearance of giving in. Which of you's given in tonight?"

Something in Lawson had once attracted him: a clarity of mind, an attitude to things and to people which fixed the reality of your relationship with them and theirs with you. Now, Ramsay told himself, what had once seemed intelligent in Lawson looked slick. You couldn't, he thought, reduce his and Craig's mutual antagonism to a simple definition: battle, giving in. He knew in his bones that there was more to it than that. He could not attempt, as Lawson had, to describe it. But Lawson was a man who described everything. He would describe the forest, he would enter the forest, but the forest would not enter him. Suddenly Ramsay felt a cause for self-congratulation that he had nominated Lawson as second-in-command of the force. It was Lawson's natural role in life.

He said to Lawson, "Neither of us has given in. Unless you call a compromise giving in."

"It is. Each side gives a bit. What did Craig give to you?"

"Sanction to go on to Khudabad."

"Where the hell's that?"

Ramsay shoved the map at him. "Where the pencil ring is."

Quicker than Craig with a map, Lawson said, "Good lord! It's miles away."

"Only twenty-five."

Lawson looked up. He really looked pretty ill.

"Another two days' forced-march?"

Ramsay shook his head. "No. We're doing it all in one day. Ten minutes' halt every hour."

"Tomorrow?"

Ramsay looked at his watch. "Today."

"Then what have *you* given in to Craig over?"

"Just that. To do it all in one day. He'll let me go to Khudabad if I speed it up."

"You're not going to be very popular."

"No."

Lawson's lips stretched over his teeth. A death-head grin. Ramsay took the map from him.

"Unless," Lawson said, "you make it clear the twenty-five-mile slog is Craig's idea."

"It's my idea."

"It's Craig's price. Between you you'll have our guts. Go on then. Reveille 0400. It's nearly that now. Get your finger out, Bob."

A hard knot constricted Ramsay's chest. He wanted to strike Lawson. But that is temper, he explained to himself, temper, personal resentment of personal criticism. These were not within the terms of reference.

"Warn Parker," he reminded. "Make a note of that. 0430 hours, platoon commanders for orders group. 0445—breakfast. 0515 strike camp. 0600 move off. That's the main time-table. The next is your pigeon."

"Shoot."

"Mules will carry minimum loads of token ammunition and mule-feed only. My guess is from the way we've worked them they won't be in Khudabad until the following morning. We'll see. Put them in the charge of the men who've been most successful with them in the last four days."

"That's be Haines, Rossiter——"

Ramsay interrupted him. "I'll leave it to you. Now. Rations. Each man to carry two days' dry rations and full water-bottle. Rations must be drawn by sections between breakfast and 0545. Ensure that all spare rations go back in the ration truck to the school. The truck must leave with the excess rations and any sick not later than 0600. I want it back in the school before Blake and his men are on the road."

"Who's Blake?"

"The enemy commander."

"Are they marching?"

"Not according to Craig. They're coming by lorry, but they

may send advance parties to direct them in and I don't want our returning ration truck to be seen coming on to the main road at the junction. It'd give away which side of the hills we are at the moment."

"Does the ration truck ever come back to us in this scheme?"

Again Ramsay controlled his impulse. "It comes back as an aeroplane. It drops four days' rations at Khudabad tomorrow night."

"Tonight, that is, seeing that it's tomorrow now."

"As you say. The ration truck should be back in the school at 0900 hours. Give the driver an indent for four days' dry rations and a request to the adjutant to see that the truck leaves for Khudabad at 1600 hours. It's about fifty-five miles he has to go all told. I reckon he'll average twenty miles an hour, taking into account the probable state of the road between here and Khudabad. He should reach Khudabad at 1900 hours, when it's dark."

"Must it be dark?"

"We shouldn't have an airdrop so close to the enemy in broad daylight."

"Is there any special significance about a drop of four days' rations?"

"It's the time I expect to be in the jungle."

Lawson pursed his lips. "Do we *carry* four days apiece?"

"We carry two. The mules'll take the other two. But of course," Ramsay paused, "—my plans may change."

"What about water?" Lawson's voice was acid.

"The water wagon will go with the ration truck and comes back with it to Khudabad for the drop."

"That's very civilized. I thought perhaps we'd get water from a village well or something."

"We would, if I had my way. Get it from a well and boil it."

"Won't Craig play?"

"The school won't play."

"What about the four days in the jungle?"

"Mules. And ingenuity. Or rain."

"I see. Well. That all?"

"More or less. Order of march, 10 platoon, headquarters group, 11 platoon, mule train, 12 platoon." Ramsay threw the pencil down. "Check with Parker. Then you'd better get some kip."

"Right. Good night then."

"One more thing. This tent can go back with the store truck."

Lawson stared. "You sleeping rough?"

"Not tonight," Ramsay replied. "After tonight."

Lawson said, "With the force commander sleeping rough it sounds as if the rest of us are for it." Again the grin, and the death-mask. "Good night again."

The flap dropped behind him.

Ramsay took off his boots. He turned the lantern down to an orange-blue glimmer. For a moment he stood in the darkness, his stockinged feet punished by the rough earth and pebbles which were the floor. Fulfilment burst inside him like a voice crying aloud.

He lay down and slept and dreamed no dream.

Craig (2)

THE MARCH to Khudabad through the heat of a summer day beat them to their knees. They trudged at three miles an hour, steadily in the early stages, then with a determined show of spirit. The last ten miles brought despair. Those who had drunk all their water grew hollow and hopeless, those who had drunk sparingly fought temptation, as bitter an enemy as thirst. Defeat, for them, was measured drop by drop.

At first Craig leap-frogged the column of march in the truck; drove a mile, waited, watched the men go past spaced out in sections on alternate sides of the road—10 platoon, Ramsay's command group, 11 platoon, the mule train, 12 platoon—then drove forward again, past them, to the next point a mile ahead. At ten minutes to each hour they halted. At ten minutes to twelve, when they had covered fifteen miles, they fell out for sixty minutes and ate hard tack with dry mouths.

Craig watched their surreptitious drinking. He warned Ramsay, "There's a lot of tilted water-bottles. One or two look empty already."

"Yes, sir. But they know the rules. If they've forgotten they'll have remembered them by five o'clock." Ramsay spoke thickly. His lips were dry, cracked, with encrusted saliva yellow in the corners.

Craig said, "Yes. The worst of the day is to come." He looked up at the white-hot sky and the sweat which had lain trapped in the folded skin of his throat trickled down his neck. His eyes stung. He lowered his head and looked at Ramsay, then at where Ramsay was looking. A man clapped the cork back on an empty bottle.

"Perhaps," Ramsay said, "they hope for a miracle."

"In the place of God?"

"An appropriate place, sir." Ramsay's tongue seemed too dry to get round the words properly. He turned away and called Lawson. When the men heard his raised voice they moved their heads round to stare dully.

Craig thought: A miracle. They look to Ramsay to provide one. They don't expect one, but they look to him, the only source of a miracle.

Ramsay looked round and said, "What, sir?"

Craig said, "I didn't speak," knew instantly that he had spoken, that he had spoken his thought aloud. He looked beyond Ramsay. A sprawled cadet gazed at him oddly. Fatigue and memory caught him: I'm past it. John died a year ago today.

He said to Ramsay, "I'll march this last ten miles. You take the truck and recce Khudabad."

"No, sir. But I'd like to send Lawson."

"Well, then. Yes, send Lawson."

He joined them to listen to their conversation.

"Take two chaps with you. Technically you lay out the dropping zone. White strip. Fire signal. Actually you recce a camp area. When you've done that send the truck back to lead us in."

Lawson said, "Right."

"And while you're at it fix on a sensible point where I can

send a fellow tonight to meet the ration truck and the water wagon. I'd prefer a camp this side of the village."

Thompson and Shaw joined them.

Shaw said, "Black mark for water discipline, Mr Ramsay," and laughed, as if to smother the sting.

Ramsay shrugged. "They'll learn." He spoke to Craig. "Should an Umpire go with Lawson?"

Craig said, "Want a ride, Sar-Major?"

"I could use one, sir."

"Accompany the second-in-command to Khudabad, then."

Shaw said, "Thompson's luck, eh?" and wandered back to where the mules stood stupefied in the scant shade a copse gave them. The hills crowded their right shoulders, but to the left of the road the trees thinned and the plain dazzled.

A miracle. The word stuck in Craig's mind. He went to the truck and scrabbled inside for his water-bottle. He clipped it to his belt and told the driver in Urdu, "I'm walking to Khudabad." The driver grinned.

An hour after noon the whistle brought them stiff-legged to their feet to form up in line of march. A second blast on the whistle set them off on the ten miles to Khudabad. Craig waited until the mule train reached the spot on which he stood, then he fell in step with Sergeant Shaw.

"What shape are these animals in, Shaw?"

"They'll last, sir. We ought to give 'em a rest tomorrow, though. They're too fat. The school don't exercise 'em enough."

"Don't let the boys force them, then. If the mule train falls behind we'll blame the school and not the men."

"OK, sir. I'll pass the word on. But what about tomorrow, sir?"

"Rest, you mean?"

"Yes. I think young Ramsay's a bit off his nut."

"Why, Staff?"

"Dragging us all this way south. By the time he gets back to the river we'll be on our knees. The other side'll wipe us up."

Craig thought, then said, "Perhaps the battle itself isn't important."

"No, sir."

Craig said, "Keep an eye on the mules."

He increased his pace, left Shaw behind, moved steadily forward past the three spaced files of 11 platoon towards Ramsay's command group.

Fifteen minutes past one: 1315 hours. A year ago they had buried their dead, were lifting John Ramsay on to the makeshift stretcher. The driving rain, filtered through the roof of the forest, soaked onto their bent backs, gathered on John's upturned face. Whenever they paused for a rest Craig sat by the stretcher. It was two hours before John spoke, and Craig had to lean close to hear.

How many?

How many what, old chap?

And John had replied: Dead, dead.

His eyes focused slowly on Craig. Craig lied: None of us, John. Just the Jap got you

The eyes had closed then. A wave of pain must have come, flushing hot and sharp from the central part of his stomach, escaping through the slack, open mouth, until the barrier of teeth closed and imprisoned it, sent it back to arch through the body and galvanize arms and fists.

Take it easy, old chap.

The spasm over, John said: Leave me here. Don't take me any farther.

Quiet, old man. Soon have you home. Soon have you fixed up.

And John had lain quiet; too quiet. Craig noticed his right hand was moving oddly. Clenched on his chest it slowly extended until the fingers were splayed and flattened to his body, and then it moved, no more than a fraction of an inch at a time, downwards, slightly to the side. Craig watched, thought at first that John moved his hand to explore the extent of his wound, until the area of exploration centred upon a point below his waist, on the outer side of his right thigh. He was feeling for his revolver. His hand traced the growth of his panic at finding it gone. Craig took the trembling hand suddenly, firmly, and then John cried out: Give it me! Give it me! Finish me off!

Craig said: Take it easy. And John grew still again as though, Craig remembered, he had removed himself from the inadequacy of those who were not in pain.

The sun blazed. The hills receded, moved forward, grew dark, glittered in the scorched retinas of Craig's eyes. When Ramsay came to where Craig sprawled at the halt he came as a black form shaped like a man, moving in a world of yellow light. As Ramsay emerged from the black shape the world behind him darkened as if in the reflection of a fire of mauve flame.

"Are we on schedule, Ramsay?"

"Yes, sir. We've done five miles in two laps of fifty minutes."

"So we'll be in Khudabad by five o'clock."

"Yes. We ought to be."

Craig thought: We bivouacked at 1700 hours. The rain stopped then. Then darkness. In the darkness John died.

He said, "Time to move on?"

"A minute to go."

"Give me a hand up."

He took Ramsay's proffered hand, held it briefly before tightening his grasp to lever himself up. When he was on his feet he loosened his grip and Ramsay removed his hand, rested it on the revolver holster which was slung from his belt.

The cadet commanding 10 platoon came down the road. He spoke to Ramsay.

"Everett looks a bit dicky, Bob."

"What's the matter with him?"

"He says he's all right, but he looks done in to me."

"Tell him to fall out and wait for the mule train."

"OK. Can he load his equipment on one of the mules?"

"If it helps him. And if the mule doesn't object."

Ramsay looked at his watch, called to the cadet deputizing for Lawson.

The whistle blew.

As headquarters group marched past Everett, Ramsay paused, went over to him. Craig waited.

Everett said, "Sorry about this." There were black shadows under his eyes. His mouth was swollen.

"Join up with the mules. If you still can't make it, wait for the ration truck. But it's only another five miles."

"I'll make it with the mules."

Ramsey suddenly bent down and shook Everett's water-bottle. Everett stared at him, unmoved.

Ramsay said, "Got a handkerchief?"

Everett hesitated, then groped in his trouser pocket.

"Yes."

"Give it here."

Ramsay took the limp square of khaki cotton, unscrewed his own water-bottle, carefully wetted it until the handkerchief was soaked.

"Hold it over your mouth."

Everett took it. He seemed to find it difficult to look at Ramsay. He said, "Thanks," turned away with the handkerchief pressed over the lower part of his face, his eyes closed.

Ramsay bent down again, picked up Everett's pack, slung it over his shoulder. Everett called out, "I can manage it, Bob," but Ramsay ignored him, rejoined Craig.

11 platoon were almost upon them. Ramsay struck up a stiff pace. Headquarters group was already some distance ahead.

Craig, packless, said, "I'll take that pack, Ramsay."

"You're not here, sir."

"What?"

"You're an Umpire, not a member of the column."

Craig said nothing for several paces. "He could have managed it himself, you know."

"He'd have loaded one of the mules with it. I was thinking of the mule's comfort, not Everett's."

At ten minutes to four they halted for the last time. Now there was no shade along the road. Ramsay shook himself free of Everett's pack and his own pack, felt inside his tunic, massaged his shoulder.

Craig said, "What would you have done with Everett if there'd been no mule train, and no ration truck?"

Ramsay continued the rubbing movements. "Nothing, sir."

"What I mean—and take this as an Umpire's question— what I mean is, if this had been an actual operation and you'd been as you are now supposed to be, miles in front of your own lines and probably within territory patrolled by the enemy, what would you do about a man falling out like Everett?"

"It wouldn't be like Everett."

"What do you mean?"

"Everett would have had to be much nearer total exhaustion to want to fall out in those circumstances. If he'd been really far gone I'd have just had to leave him. And *if* he'd been so far gone it wouldn't have been any loss to me. He'd have been no use, as I see it."

"Suppose he'd been wounded?"

Ramsay had slipped his tunic away from his shoulder. Absently he fingered the deep weal which the strap of the pack had bitten into the flesh. He asked, "Seriously wounded?"

"Yes. Unable to walk."

"Perhaps a couple of chaps would have helped him into Khudabad."

"You'd depend on men volunteering to do that?"

"No." A pause. "No. I think I'd have to order it."

"Why? If he were badly wounded you'd probably only be taking him to Khudabad to die."

"I might have laid on the evacuation of wounded by light aircraft. I'd try and get one to take Everett out from Khudabad."

"Then let's put it this way. For what reason would you have laid on or tried to lay on the evacuation of wounded men by air, or conceivably by road?—perhaps we could visualize an ambulance unit operating forward to Khudabad especially for you. But why would you have laid evacuation on?"

Ramsay readjusted his tunic, looked at Craig. "A badly wounded man is likely to be a total loss, but you'd evacuate him if you could, because anything else would lower the morale of the fit men."

"Explain why it would lower their morale."

Ramsay said, "If you have to leave a badly wounded man behind on his own, the others would worry about being wounded themselves. If they knew they'd be looked after they'd worry less. But if they worry their morale goes down and they don't do their job properly."

Craig turned his head away. He said to himself: Yes, that is the principle. That is quite clear. Aloud he said, "What about yourself, Ramsay, as commander? Would your morale go down if you thought a bad wound meant your being left in the jungle?"

"A commander is in a special position, I think, sir."

"Explain that position."

After a moment or two Ramsay said, "In the last resort a commanding officer has to rely on himself."

Craig looked at him sharply. "My words," he said.

"Yes, sir. It's what you said when we first talked about John."

"My words impressed themselves on you, then?"

"Yes, I think so. I understand the meaning better now. My own idea was that each man had to rely on himself. You disputed that, if you remember, and then said this about self-reliance only really applying to the commander."

Craig said, "And how would this self-reliance help you as a badly wounded commander in danger of being left in the jungle?"

"A badly wounded commander is no longer capable of commanding. My job would have finished. The next chap would take over."

"And you?"

"I'd be his responsibility, sir."

Craig smiled. His cracked lips hurt. "You make it all sound very mechanical, as if people weren't involved at all."

On the last lap Craig walked some distance behind Ramsay. Ramsay had sent his command group ahead to make contact with Lawson and marched alone in the middle of the road, his figure hunched against the weight of his two packs. Craig kept his eyes fixed on Ramsay, kept in step with him, watched for the moment when Ramsey swung Everett's pack from one shoulder to the other. After a while Craig began to count the number of paces he took between Ramsay's change from one shoulder to the other, realized after two changes that Ramsay was counting as well, setting himself the discipline of taking one hundred and fifty steps before moving the pack. As Craig went on counting he received an impression of the increasing weight, of the extra demand on his body and mind each stint of one hundred and fifty steps exacted, until it seemed to him that he watched Ramsay being punished, and in the lower reach of his consciousness a flame of pity and tenderness sprang up and he suddenly asked himself: Why am I doing this to Ramsay?

And then: What am I doing to Ramsay?

He watched Ramsay marching alone ahead. He counted the paces they took in unison. The question could no longer be answered by evasion. He had clearly, at last, to ask himself: What am I doing to Ramsay? And the answer could no longer be hidden away in that part of him where it had lain. It had been smoked out. Here it was, in its naked simplicity: I am helping Ramsay to destroy himself as a man. I am helping him to be alone in the forest to kill, and that will be the end of him as a man, because that is what man is forbidden.

They marched another one hundred and fifty paces. Ramsay swung the pack to his other shoulder. The first question was asked again: Why am I doing this to Ramsay? Why am I doing this to Ramsay? His eyes fixed on Ramsay's heavy ammunition boots, the web gaiters, the trousers bagged over the gaiters, the tight buttocks and the ends of the diagonal shoulder-straps hanging below the webbing-belt which supported the jogging water-bottle on one side and the revolver holster on the other, the neat square pack with its inch of groundsheet showing beneath the flap, the shaved neck exposed by the tunic collar pulled down by the weight of the pack, the topee, the steady mechanical plod, and, ahead of Ramsay, a column of identical figures, identical except for the slung rifle in place of a revolver and a sheathed bayonet dancing at the hip. Why am I doing this to Ramsay?

And the answer came up to Craig from the long road upon which one hundred exhausted men scuffed up the dust and down from the sky which imprisoned them in a bowl of heat: Because we are men bent on destruction, who fear destruction, who wish to survive, who therefore need a man to lead us who is past destroying, beyond survival, a man stronger even than John Ramsay. We take what material is offered and shape it for our safety.

The flame of tenderness died. Ramsay had helped Everett, whatever he had said, whatever name he had put to it. Something of compassion had informed his action. That way lay failure. It was as important to Craig, now, that Ramsay should not fail as it had once been important that John should not die.

Ramsay (2)

THE FIRST sight of Khudabad in the distance produced in him a disappointment so tangible that he felt it like a hand inside his belly knotting itself into a fist. He tried to ignore it in the way he had tried to ignore the thought of Everett and of what he had done for Everett; as before, he failed.

He ordered the signal to halt, walked on with Craig just behind him until he came to Lawson who had stopped the truck a little way down the road and then got out to meet them. Lawson had come alone with the driver.

"Where are the others?" Ramsay asked.

"In Khudabad."

"*In* Khudabad?"

Lawson said, "Yes, hop in, I'll show you. There's room for everybody in the village."

Ramsay felt irritation stab at the surface of his skin. He snapped at Lawson, "I don't want them *in* the village. I want 'em outside, in a proper bivouac."

Lawson grinned. "No need to bivouac. Khudabad's deserted. Empty. Dead as a doornail."

Behind him Ramsay heard Craig say, "Did you say empty, Lawson?"

"Yes, sir. It looks as if the whole population just cleared off one day. Everything's gone to wrack and ruin, but the huts are better than sleeping in the open."

Craig said, "Let's go and see it." He climbed into the truck. Lawson got in the back.

Ramsay called Lawson's deputy.

"Let the column fall out here. I'll send back when I'm ready."

He joined Lawson behind Craig and the driver. Lawson was describing things to Craig and Craig was saying, "Perhaps there was an epidemic."

The truck turned, gathered speed. Through the pall of raised dust Ramsay could see Lawson's deputy staring after them and behind the deputy the column, scattered about the roadside.

They drove for about half a mile. The road they were on seemed to continue westwards towards the hill spur and was, no doubt, the western arm of the road which encircled the Chota Bandar. The village of Khudabad lay on the T junction where the road which came up from the south joined the first at right angles. The truck stopped at the junction, outside a crumbling mud hut. On the opposite side of the road there was a stagnant tank, a stretch of sparsely grassed *maidan* and then the outer fringes of scrub, the rougher country which rolled itself up into the forested hills.

Ramsay crossed the road and looked at the tank. On this side there were flattened stones at the water's edge where women had washed the family's clothing. He rejoined the others.

It was true. The place was derelict: a dozen huts of varying shape and size, ravaged by sun and rain. At the last of the huts they entered through the open doorway. The one room opened on to a smaller, a kitchen with blackened floor and wall. The door of the kitchen opened on to a mud-walled compound. There was nothing there that had been left behind to define an existence, a way of life.

They returned to the roadway, walked back to the T junction. Thompson was chatting to the driver.

Ramsay said to Lawson, "Where's your dropping zone?"

"There on the maidan."

"Right." He turned to Craig. "I'm calling an O group. Can Lawson fetch the platoon commanders in the truck, sir?"

"Of course."

"Get them, will you?"

Lawson nodded. "Right."

"And tell 10 platoon commander to get his column up here."

"Not 11 or 12?"

"No. They stay put for a while."

When Lawson had gone Craig said, "Are you going to use the village?"

"Only for 10 platoon."

"Why?"

"Two reasons, sir. I don't want us all bunched here. And I don't like the proximity of that tank."

"Why?"

"Malaria, sir. I want to hold the village, but only with a reserve platoon."

Craig nodded. "Don't tell me any more. I'll listen to your O group."

The truck came back. Lawson got out. 10, 11 and 12 platoon commanders followed. They looked round. One said, "Crikey! Dead man's gulch."

Ramsay said, "Right. Situation. Imagine we've come up that road." He pointed down the village street to the south. "The village is deserted. That might be due to a local epidemic or enemy action."

"Maybe the landlord put the rent up——"

"Moonlight flit on a major scale."

They laughed, licked their lips with dry tongues.

Ramsay turned to 10 platoon commander. "As we reached the village I dropped you off to get astride the road and guard our rear. You can put your chaps in the huts, but in the hours of daylight you must keep them under cover. I don't want 'em swanning about in the open. The road junction is a good navigation-fix, so you can expect enemy aircraft overhead. Observe strict track discipline everybody, please."

"OK, Bob. What's my area?"

"You can command 180 degrees south of this road we're on, from the village itself. Apart from that, standing as you are now, in front of you you've got the open space beyond the tank. That's the DZ for the drop tonight, and I'm making it your responsibility."

"That means I deal with the ration and water trucks when they come in?"

"Yes. But I want you to set up your recognition signals on the DZ itself."

"Set up fires, you mean?"

"Yes."

"And light 'em?"

"Why not? Light them when you hear the aircraft."

"When the old 30-cwt changes gear. OK, Bob. What about the road?"

"The road we've just come down is your sector too. In fact you've got an arc described from north of the maidan right round to and inclusive of the road."

"Limit?"

"Two hundred yards from this spot." Ramsay turned to the commander of 11 platoon. "You go into the scrub."

"My luck."

"Fix your right boundary north of the maidan with 10 platoon. I want you in a 90 degree arc from north of the maidan round to that first hill feature there. 12 platoon——"

"Yes, Bob."

"Fix your right boundary with 11 platoon at the hill feature and take the scrub in an arc back to the road on the other side of the junction, two hundred yards west of this spot."

"Where'll your command group be, Ramsay?"

Ramsay turned to Craig: "I'm just going to tell them, sir." He turned back to the three cadets. "I'll be just inside the scrub, there—due north of the road junction."

Lawson said, "And the commissariat?"

"Commissariat and mules will go in the command group perimeter. The collecting party on the DZ would normally cart the stuff quite easily from DZ to commissariat. As it is they'll have to hump it from the truck here."

He paused before saying the next word.

"Water."

The air was suddenly drier, parched beyond imagination.

"I've indented for water in the drop. It'll come in the water wagon, of course. Platoon'll fill water-bottles by sections—supposedly from the commissariat—actually from the water wagon here. Two men from each section will bring their section's water-bottles when they get the word. Any questions?"

"Yes, Bob. What about konner?"

"No hot meal tonight, I'm afraid."

"Crikey. Dry fodder again."

"Now, get your chaps in before it's dark. Brew up under section arrangements. Perimeter guards fron nightfall and no fires except the DZ fire. Stand to, 0430 to 0500. O group at 0600. Better get moving."

"Can we go back in the Umpire's truck?"

Craig said, "Yes, just 11 and 12 platoon commanders. 10 platoon's already on the way, isn't it?"

10 platoon commander said, "Yes, sir. They're coming now."

Craig said to Thompson, "You stay here in the village, Sar-Major, and keep an eye on this lot. I'll watch out for the others."

Ramsay, remembering, called suddenly, "One more thing."

The three platoon commanders waited.

"This is the forming-up point. We begin properly now."

When darkness came there was a measure of privacy. He had made himself a rough shelter of branches covered by a groundsheet and crawled into it now to light the hurricane lamp and look once more at the map. Outside they were having trouble with the mules. All around him was the sound of hard earth broken up by pick-axes as slit trenches were dug; sometimes a soft sound, sometimes metallic as axe-point met stone.

A voice said, "Char up, Bob." He turned, saw the face of the cadet detailed as command group runner at the opening of his shelter.

"Thanks, shove it in." A mess tin was pushed towards him. Some of the tea slopped, congealed darkly into the dry earth floor.

"Is Everett back?"

"Yeah. Came in with the mules."

"I didn't see him with them."

"Well, he's back. Bit behind the mules. Seems OK though." The cadet waited. "That all, Bob?"

"Yes. Thanks for the char."

He drank. It burnt his swollen lips, drew the sweat into his face. When he had got used to the burning sensation he found that the tea tasted of wood smoke.

He put the mess tin down when it was empty, leaned back on one elbow, looked again at the map, closed his eyes. For one brief, startling moment he thought: I'm whacked, had it. The word responsibility formed itself in his mind, first as the word itself only, than as the particular idea the word conveyed. He opened his eyes. The map stared back at him.

Water, he thought. Food. One hundred men. Fifteen miles of tortuous switchback jungle between us and the river.

A cheer went up.

He crawled out of his shelter. The runner came up and shouted, "They've lit the DZ fires."

Ramsay, upright, saw the yellow flames sprouting. He looked at his watch. 1945 hours. He strained his ears to catch the growl of the ration truck and water wagon, but the camp was jubilant, yelling its appreciation of the drama.

He bumped into someone. "Tell 'em to pipe down," he said, and brushed the man away. As he stumbled through the scrub he yelled, "Cut it out! Cut it out!" and gradually he was aware of his voice impinging on a growing silence and then he could hear the trucks.

There was a huddle of men on the road. More were coming to join them.

"Get the hell back," he shouted. Someone said, "Collecting party, Bob." And he repeated, "Get the hell back." As they went he called, "Platoon commander!" and then saw the remaining man lift a hand. "Here, Bob."

"It looks and sounds just like a bloody school treat. Christ, listen to it." The cheering had sparked again on the other side of the scrub.

"Oh, shove it, Bob."

"Shove what?"

"Your bloody exercise."

The headlights caught them. Ducking his head down Ramsay saw that the collecting party were within earshot. He said, "We'll go into that later. Let's concentrate on this lot."

"Why go into it later? Why not now?"

Ramsay raised his voice. "Because the rest of the company's more interested in what's in the trucks than in your opinion of my bloody exercise." He turned away. The 30-cwt dipped its headlight, slowed. He stood in the road and beckoned it on, indicating with a sweep of his arm that it should turn left into the south road.

A mile back the water wagon trundled in its wake.

Ramsay's runner was at his elbow suddenly. He turned, grateful for the man's initiative.

"Any chore, Bob?"

"Thanks. Get this chap parked fifty yards down the road and the water wagon in behind it, so's we can use its headlight and see what we're about."

"Right, Bob."

"And then go round the platoons and tell them to send their water fatigues along."

The runner jumped on the cabin step as the truck wheeled slowly round at the junction, shouted instructions in bad Urdu. Ramsay watched the truck turn. Because he did so he saw the white-clothed figure in the back.

He told 10 platoon commander to await the water wagon before sending the collecting party to off-load. Now he went slowly down the street to where the 30-cwt truck had just come to a halt. The runner walked back towards him, but the figure in the back of the truck had not moved.

Ramsay said, "OK. Grab the water wagon when it arrives," and then went on alone. The driver had climbed down from the cabin, stood now, was silhouetted against the glow of the sidelights, made stretching movements. Ramsay reached the truck, went straight to the driver.

"Who've you got in the back?"

"Sahib?"

He spoke in Urdu. "In the back of the lorry there is a passenger."

"Yes, sir. I had forgotten."

The driver called out, "Ai!" and went round to the back of the truck. Ramsay went with him. The white-clad figure had one leg over the back board. The driver helped him down and said, "The sahib is asking about you." The man replied too fluently for Ramsay to catch the full sense of it, but what he understood was innocent enough.

The man was broad-shouldered, taller than Ramsay. He wore a white *dhoti* and homespun shirt. In the luminous dark his skin was blue-black.

Ramsay said, still in Urdu, "This is a military lorry. Why do you travel in it?" The pungent smell of betel-nut came from the man.

"Sahib, I was a long way from home. Your driver stopped. I asked him, 'Where are you going?'" he said, and more which Ramsay could not keep track of.

"Please speak slowly. I understand only the language of the military. Do you speak English?"

"Little English."

"What is your occupation?"

"I am a poor merchant."

The man had begun to grin. Suddenly he was disclosed fully by the headlamp of the water wagon which had rounded the corner. The man shielded his eyes, lowered his head. Ramsay saw the string round his neck.

The water wagon stopped. Ramsay's runner called out, "OK, Bob?"

"OK. Tell him to keep his lights on." He smiled at the man. "We are going to unload the lorry. Have you any luggage?"

"No, sahib."

"Where have you come from?"

The man mentioned the town which gave the school its name but added something which Ramsay interpreted as meaning he did not live there, but had had business there.

"And was your business successful?"

The collecting party came down the street. The man eyed Ramsay.

"No, sir. I lost all my money. Your driver took pity on me when he saw me walking in the dust of the road."

Ramsay waited. When the collecting party arrived they gathered round and waited too. Someone said, "Who's this? Joe Cooch?"

Ramsay said, "A chap who cadged a lift."

"Hope he's not scoffed all the grub."

"Come on, Bob. What are we waiting for?"

Ramsay said, "To find out more about him."

The man still grinned.

Ramsay said, "Where did my driver pick you up?"

"Many miles away."

Ramsay turned to the driver. "What did he ask of you?"

"He asked me where I was going, sahib."

"And you told him you were going to Khudabad?"

"Yes, sir."

"What did he say then?"

"He said that he lived in Khudabad."

A cadet said, "Don't any of them speak English?"

Ramsay said over his shoulder. "This chap lives in Khudabad."

"The only one then. What's he do for a biwi?"

Ramsay put a hand on the man's shoulder. "This is a strange story, brother, because nobody lives in Khudabad. I do not think that you live in Khudabad. I think that you live in the Company of Lieutenant Blake sahib." He moved his hand and dragged at the string round the man's neck. On the end of it was the military identity disc.

The man roared with laughter and said in English, "Now I'm a prisoner of war, sahib, and must be treated in accordance with the rules of International Red Cross, isn't it?"

"I say," someone said. "He's a —ing spy," and they joined their laughter to his.

Their positions were reversed. In his tent Craig sat with the map spread on top of a box, weighted on one of its corners by the lighted hurricane. Ramsay crouched on the stool.

Craig said, "How do you know it's one of Blake's men?"

"He admits it. His name is Baksh. Havildar Rahman Baksh."

"Does Blake know he's here?"

"Yes, sir." He saw his careful plans topple, scatter like the bricks he played with when a kid. He said, "The bloody bastard put a watch on both road junctions to keep a lookout for our ration truck and check which road it took."

"And Havildar Baksh was one of these lookouts?"

"Yes, sir."

Lines of concentration appeared on Craig's forehead. Ramsay waited. Presently Craig said, "Surely all Blake will know at this moment is that Havildar Baksh has failed to return from his post at the road junction nearer the school? In other words, Ramsay, Blake can't know Baksh is here. He can only guess that Baksh may have cadged a lift on the truck which was on its way to some point on the road to Nanyaganj or beyond. He may guess at Khudabad from studying the map. But he can't *know*. Alternatively he may think his Havildar has gone absent without leave."

Again Ramsay waited. Craig was looking at him, half smiling. Craig had failed to ask the obvious question. Ramsay considered this failure. Contempt for Craig's error warmed the pleasure he could feel now, in retrospect, in his surer grasp of the situation.

He said, "That would be right if Baksh had been alone at the junction, but according to the driver he wasn't. After talking to Baksh I asked the driver whether he'd been alone and the driver said there was another chap waiting with him, but that according to Baksh the other chap didn't want to come to Khudabad."

"Does Baksh admit that?"

"No. But you can see he's lying. Blake posted a couple of chaps together, dressed in civilian clothes. Baksh's pal obviously went back and told Blake that our truck was headed for here."

"I see. But why is Baksh here? What does he hope to do?"

"I've talked to him about that, sir. In the first place he didn't expect to be found out. In the second place he thought he'd wander round like a friendly villager, find out all he could about where and when we were going, then get a lift back in the truck tomorrow."

"He was taking a chance."

"I think that's by the way, sir. What I don't like is Blake's cheating. For the purpose of the exercise the ration truck didn't exist. It was an aeroplane coming up from the south, not a

30-cwt coming down the road giving lifts to Blake's men dressed as civvies—Blake's men dressed as civvies and stuck miles from where Blake's men are *supposed* to be stuck."

"I agree, Ramsay."

"It's a lot of useless nonsense, I suppose, but I lodge a formal protest to the Chief Umpire."

"I note your protest and endorse it. What practical step do you propose to take?"

"I'm forced to turn Baksh's presence into a situation. It's an unsatisfactory situation, because Blake knows for sure where Baksh has been captured."

"You'll hold him prisoner, then?"

"With your permission."

"You have my permission. What it the situation you've evolved?"

"That he's a villager working for the enemy. We caught him nosing around, but too late to stop him sending a message back about us arriving here."

"That's logical. What do you do, 'Shoot' him?"

"No, sir."

"What then?"

"Force him to march with us."

"In reality?"

"Yes." Ramsay paused, uncertain of Craig's reaction, but determined. "Baksh is wearing only sandals on bare feet."

"That'll be a bit hard on him, won't it?"

"He looks tough enough. He'll need to be, too. Blake didn't supply him with rations."

He watched Craig's face, believed there was wariness in Craig's smile.

Craig said, "What does that imply?"

"That he'll eat and drink what he can beg. Or what the rest of us are prepared to give up from our supplies."

Suddenly there was a picture of himself giving water to Everett. It fused with the real picture of Craig staring at him and then, unbidden, came a memory of his brother; and the tent was a lamplit island in a dark world with himself and Craig the only people alive in it and contempt for Craig died and left in its place contempt for himself, so that he needed

Craig to share the weight of it, to ease it away like a burden eased from his shoulders.

"You mean Baksh will go hungry and thirsty?"

He could read nothing into Craig's expression or tone of voice. He said, "I expect so."

Craig looked down at the map, as though in denial, and Ramsay thought of Craig saying, Give me a hand up, of the contact of their hands, of Craig's weight. He opened his mind to receive Craig's denial, to receive Craig, consider with him the idea of Baksh's privation. He thought: Unless you disapprove: but said, "Do you disapprove?" And Craig turned his eyes on him and replied, "*You're* the commander of Ramforce. You must make your own decisions."

Silence expanded between them. In it Craig seemed to grow larger, himself smaller.

He lay in the darkness of his bivouac. A hand had shaken him by the ankles and a voice said, "They're standing to, Bob." He had come from nothing to the surface of the new day. Cramp and cold brought him back into his body. The day and his body fused and became one, separated by sleep from the full memory of yesterday.

The hand shook his ankles again, the voice said, "OK, Bob?"

"Thanks."

His mouth was bitter with a taste like metal. He felt for his water-bottle, found and uncorked it and lifted it to his lips. He kept the water in his mouth until it had softened the back of his throat and he could regulate the swallowing of it.

There was something wrong with his eyes. Light stabbed spasmodically. He let his lids drop. The light was not there except as a reflection from outside. Here it comes. One. Two. A long darkness. He raised the lids. Three. The light was there again, but with a feeling of actuality and distance in it. Four. Five. He struggled out of the shelter and stood up. There was no light. But then it flickered again along the south-west horizon. His urban mind described it: Like an electric railway, far off.

He walked through the scrub to the open land, saw like a

cat in the dark. The eastern horizon was grey-green, the stars pale there, but bright above him. In the south-west they were invisible. The sheet lightning spread with a regularity he now found, fully awake, a cause for wonder. Once he believed he heard the rumble of thunder. A picket-guard challenged him. The disembodied voice diminished the size and shape of the night, brought him again to the centre of his own world. The hours of sleep which had separated him from it telescoped. The world. Oblivion. The world again, and Craig.

He began his tour of the perimeter, and as he went pride grew within a sense of corporate safety because his world, his circle of land, was awake, alert, sensitive. A kind of love, an excitement at the pattern his will had imposed upon the ground, moved him, hardened him. He felt immensely powerful, the sum of all of them, the whole of which they were only parts.

He remembered Craig's words: You make it all sound very mechanical, as if people weren't involved at all. And then he felt bigger than Craig, as though he had reached a conclusion Craig knew to be the right conclusion, but from which he retreated.

He stood still, the better to shoulder, finally, his responsibility. He understood it to be a responsibility which Craig had seen he was cut out to bear. He tried to recapture the self-contempt which had bitten into him, in order to understand its nature. It had been to do with Baksh and, perversely, Everett.

The eastern horizon had whitened, the stunted trees and bush which formed the scrub had achieved substance, a grey dimension out of the night. His land was growing to definition and to it Baksh's presence was a threat. Not Baksh. Baksh's presence.

And Everett? Everett was one of the parts.

I needed the part, Ramsay told himself. I gave Everett water, because I did not want to lose the part.

But Baksh's presence is a threat. Challenge a threat, reduce it, twist it to advantage.

If Baksh suffers, he does so because of what he represents.

There was no weight of self-contempt in these things, only

responsibility. You must make your own decisions. Craig said it. The forest speaks to you. It does not speak to me. Craig said that too.

And: There are things you can never know; only guess. John.

John had once been a part of Craig's whole. The problem reached Ramsay now, dryly, unemotionally, where before there had been pain to be considered, and imminent death. These remained, but in the background, to comfort dismay perhaps.

Image Everett. Imagine Everett in John's circumstance: Everett movable only by stretcher, up the hill, down the hill, draining the strength of the few parts which were all that were left to express the shape and course of his own action. Finish me off. A few hours left. That was all. The enemy behind. How far behind? If far enough, then getting closer because the stricken part slowed the whole, threatened the whole.

Leave him.

Shoot or leave him? If left, he might live until the enemy found him. They would come upon him, interrogate him. Which way? Scream. That way. And death after all. So shoot him now. The last expedient disguised as the last humanity.

Yes, he would shoot Everett, and the parts would incorrectly understand it as mercy and be comforted by it, climb the hill lighter, within the circle of safety he had reimposed, and when he understood that this is what had to be done, and what he would do, he told himself at last that Craig would not do it, that Craig had known it should be done to John, but had not done it; guessed that this was what Craig had been telling him right from the beginning and why, when he had needed Craig to share the weight of his self-contempt last night, Craig had failed him because the weight of his own was as much as he could bear.

Ramsay (3)

IT WAS easier to see them now for what they should be: men acting out a part allotted to them; extensions of his own limbs, himself multiplied to perform a task his single mind but not his lone body could accomplish.

He led his orders group down to the village, entered the hut which 10 platoon commander had used as his headquarters. The morning was grey, lacked the cool freshness of a new day.

"We're in for it proper," 12 platoon commander said. He stood at the entrance, watched the sky to the south-west.

Lawson came in, looked at his watch. "0605. Sorry. I'm late."

10 platoon commander shrugged. "We can't start until the Umpires get here. They're later." He had broken his own embarrassed silence. He added in a studiedly controlled voice, "I apologize for last night, Bob," and the others shuffled, embarrassed themselves now.

Ramsay had begun to take out his cigarettes. He felt detached from the men in the room, from the apology and from the offence of the night before. He held out the packet to 10 platoon commander. He said, "That's all right."

"Thanks, Bob."

The cigarette packet went round. The word would go round that the man had apologized for telling Ramsay to shove it, would follow the word that had already gone round of what the man had told Ramsay. It was because the word had gone round, reached Craig's ear already, perhaps, that the apology had been made, in fear, not in regret.

Ramsay smoked while the others talked. There was a special unreality within the larger unreality against which he fought, and this was bound up in the fact of their being cadets, in sight of their commissions. They were all of them potential leaders and preferred to do, he imagined, as they would be done by. They were easier to lead because each had to subscribe to a belief in leadership. He had less need to consider their comfort

133

than he would if they had been of the rank and file. They would endure, now, against the day they needed others to endure. And yet—and Ramsay turned suddenly to watch them—balanced against this asset was the liability of their knowledge that the enemy was no enemy, the threat only an assumed threat.

He began to feel that the room confined him, that the threat and the enemy were outside. He grew impatient waiting for Craig and Thompson and Shaw. He glanced at his notes. Lawson said, "Here they are," and then Craig was in the room, then Thompson, then Shaw, and they all stood and gradually formed a pattern of which he was the key. For a moment before he began to talk he saw himself divided, sub-divided, each of the divisions and sub-divisions turned towards a point from which a single will should have established coherence of action, but it seemed, too, that the single will had splintered, itself entered into a process of division, and he was left powerless to decide or desire to combat the thing which the room communicated. It is not real, there is no enemy, there is no threat. But as his voice issued, strong, decisive, the fragments gathered, achieved cohesion again.

"We'll begin by considering the situation." His hand moved, to his map, but his eyes were on their hands, drawn to them because each of them had touched his own map and now, when he looked at their faces, their eyes were cast down as though, for the moment, he was the map, his voice the voice of the map.

"As we're placed we're about fifteen miles due south of the area we're to examine." He gave them a map reference, waited for them to find it. "That puts you on the highest point of the Chota Bandar and we'll call it Elephant Hill."

Lawson said, "Is that its name?"

"No. It looks like an elephant's back and head. Has everybody got that?" He watched them. Even Shaw and Thompson nodded. Only Craig's head was still.

"Just north of Elephant Hill is the line of the river and on the other side of the river the line of the centre ridge. The centre ridge slopes down on its north side to the main road. My information is that the enemy in company strength commands that area. Our job is to avoid his patrols, bump his main body, destroy what we can of his force, harass his line of communication—which is the road—and bring our own force out with the minimum loss."

10 platoon commander said, "What about the rest of the enemy front—I mean what are we to imagine on his left and right flank?"

"The main enemy front is far to the east. We're approaching a part of the line which is held by the minimum number of troops. The hills and the jungle are considered sufficient obstacle to a large-scale attack by our side."

"I see. I was thinking of him getting imaginary reinforcements."

"Our information is that no considerable help could be brought in to oppose our attack in less than twelve hours. He has L of C troops in his rear. We have no intelligence reports about other troop reserves in this particular area."

"In other words, Bob, if we crack this particular lot we've got time to mess things up a bit before we have to skedaddle."

"So far as we know. The situation is always open to sudden change." Ramsay did not look at Craig, but the others did.

Craig said, "Ramsay's appreciation of the general enemy situation is a perfectly reasonable one. I don't anticipate a major, or even a minor change in it. Although, of course, there is the situation created by Mr Baksh. Will you be dealing with that, Ramsay?"

"Yes, sir."

"Carry on, then."

"Right. I'll come to Baksh presently. Meanwhile, you know the picture about the enemy, our destination, our object and our present geographical position. Let's now consider how we're placed operationally.

"We're here in Khudabad, fifteen miles from Elephant Hill as the crow flies, more like thirty miles as the ant crawls on the ground, if we go in a straight line across the grain of the hills. It's estimated that our column, plus mule train, could only average five miles a day. In other words, we're three days' march from the Elephant Hill area. Each man now holds one day's rations left over from the two days' rations drawn yesterday morning. Our airdrop of four days' rations gives us five days' rations in all. We shall consume the one day's rations today. To start our approach march tomorrow we should do so with four days' rations. Normally we might carry two days' a man and let the mules take the other two days'. But from now on the mules will carry nothing except general stores, token ammunition, their own feed and water. Each man will therefore have to carry four days' rations."

Ramsay paused. He felt Craig's intense scrutiny.

"I've got a bit of a shock for you, though. Our airlift last night wasn't wholly successful. Only three days' rations were dropped and one days' ration of tinned meat has turned out to be rotten. We shall be on half rations for four days, in consequence, but with the advantage of less to carry."

"What about water?"

"The water was all right."

"We'll be able to drink rain water, anyway. Buckets of it."

"Bob, what actually happens to the two days' rations and the 'rotten' meat? After all, we've got it here."

Shaw said, grinning, "You gotta pretend you're not carrying it."

Ramsay waited until the laughter had stopped. "We'll send it back in the ration truck."

"Old Blake'll pinch it."

"I hope an Umpire will go back with the ration truck."

Craig said, "Why, Ramsay?"

"To establish the Baksh situation with Blake."

Lawson said, "What *is* the Baksh situation?"

"I'll deal with it now." He put his map aside. "Blake knows that we're in Khudabad. I've made an official complaint to the Chief Umpire about it. I expect Blake thought it was a hell of a clever thing to do. I think it was merely lousy."

"That's putting it mildly."

Ramsay continued: "The main object of the march to Khudabad has been defeated, so we can thank Blake for that particular twenty-five mile slog." He paused to let the suggestion sink in. "I think we might find an opportunity of settling that account."

"We'll make one if we can't find one."

Ramsay said, "But to come back to Baksh. This is the situation circumstances have forced me to evolve: Baksh is a fifth columnist whom we captured and interrogated. During interrogation he broke down and admitted what he had previously denied, that is, that he had a pal who's gone off to Blake to report our presence and Baksh's capture."

They were grinning. One of them said, "How did we interrogate Mr Baksh? Beat the hell out of him, I hope."

"I imagine we only threatened physical violence."

"What else did he tell us?"

"Nothing else. He doesn't know anything else."

"Does he know exactly where Blake's got his positions?"

"He says he doesn't. We imagine he's speaking the truth. He's volunteered the information that Blake's got a company in that particular area, but we knew that already."

Lawson said, "It seems to me Blake comes off best in this particular situation. We know nothing we. didn't know, but Blake knows we exist and where we are."

Ramsay said, "Yes. But we *know* Blake knows where we are. And he still doesn't know which way we're coming."

"Which way *are* we going?"

"Just a moment——"

Craig said, "This is an orders group, gentlemen. The commander holds the floor. The questions come after."

They moved, uncomfortably, and Ramsay waited, angry with Craig because Craig has broken the spell he knew he had weaved with the names of Blake and Baksh. Through Craig's words they had come back from the illusion into the exercise.

He said, suddenly, but deliberately, "I should like to control my own orders group, sir."

He gained an impression of none but himself and Craig breathing. Shaw's mouth had fallen open. Thompson looked at Craig and then back at Ramsay, but before the Sergeant-Major could speak Ramsay said, in general, "Blake's knowledge of our position sets a problem. I'd intended to move due north for about ten miles and form a springboard a mile or two south of the river, a sort of strongpoint from which we could operate offensively in whatever direction we decided best at the time. The strongpoint or springboard would also have been a rendezvous for regrouping when we came out of the attack. The problem is—now that Blake knows we're in Khudabad, will he guess at that plan? It you were Blake at this moment what conclusions would you come to? I thought it would be useful to pool ideas."

He reached for a cigarette. The familiar knot of excitement twisted in his stomach. He had replaced the illusion Craig had shattered with a new illusion into which his second-in-command and his platoon commanders could enter, one by one, as if into himself. It needed only one of them to speak and then Craig and Thompson and Shaw would be excluded, exiled together in the unreality from which the illusion could protect the rest of them. He caught the eye of 10 platoon commander, addressed him for the first time by his Christian name.

"Tony?"

"If I were Blake?"

He smiled, safe. "If you were Blake."

"Give me a moment, Bob." He looked at his map.

"Right. Someone else." 11 platoon commander. "Paddy?"

"If I were Blake, I'd be foxed. One thing I *would* do——"

"What?"

"I'd get on to battalion or brigade, or whatever, and tell 'em there was a penetration group reported at Khudabad and ask 'em to send down an air recce or strike pretty damn quick."

"Right. You've done that. It's 0615. Baksh's pal has just got in after travelling all night and you've asked for this air recce. Now you're us again and not Blake. Baksh has told you about his pal. You estimate Blake's just got the message. What would you do?"

11 platoon commander stared back at him, then said, "Hell, get out of Khudabad and into the jungle. Is that what we're going to do?"

"Yes. 0700 we up sticks here and get well under cover a mile into the jungle." Ramsay turned to 12 platoon commander. "Angus? You're Blake again. The air recce comes back. It hasn't seen a thing. The Brigadier gets on the blower. You suggest some reinforcements. He asks you where you think he's going to get reinforcements from. It's an L of C area. The air recce put in a negative report. He reminds you of the hundred and one other times there've been similar flaps about enemy in the jungle. Finally, to cover himself in case there *is* trouble, he tells you to keep on the alert, increase your patrol activity, keep him informed."

"A helpful sort of bugger."

"That's it. So you're on your jack jones again. What do you do?"

"Get hold of Baksh's pal and give him the treatment—I take it I'm a Jap bastard?"

"Yes, you can take it you are."

"All right, then, I sharpen a bamboo stake and shove it up his arse to see if he tells the same story. He does, only more so, so I start poking a bayonet into his guts—and when it gets to the point where he says there are several hundred of you and honest he's telling the truth, I can't decide whether he's been lying all the time, but frightened to admit it, or whether there really are hundreds of you, the very idea of which scares me to death, so I cut his bloody head off."

Grinning, Ramsay said, "But what do you do then?"

"I reckon I've done enough, Bob. I sit staring at a map and wondering what happens next. I send everyone out on a patrol, then haul 'em back because I'm shit-scared stuck up there with all my men gone."

"Thanks." He caught 10 platoon commander's eye. "What've you decided, Tony?"

"I'm afraid I've been too engrossed in the picture Angus has conjured up for us to come to a decision. One thing I'm not sure of though. We know Blake knows we're here, but does he know we know?" He smiled apologetically. "If you see what I mean?"

"Yes, I do. The answer is he doesn't know we know yet. But we've created this situation about Baksh and I hope the Umpires will pass it on to Blake. He will then know we know he knows we're here."

"How do we explain that in terms of the situation?"

"Baksh's pal witnessed Baksh's capture. Blake therefore knows Baksh is in our hands. He'll be pretty certain Baksh will let on that he's sent a message through about our where-abouts."

Lawson said, "And where does that lead us?"

Ramsay said, "Tony, you raised the point. Any particular reason?"

"I'm not sure, Bob." 10 platoon commander frowned slightly. "Except that it complicates the picture for Blake." He picked up his map, stared at it, spoke again: "I think if I were Blake, merely knowing you were in Khudabad I'd guess you'd approach more or less direct through the jungle, if only because the jungle gives cover, and there isn't much point in going through the jungle to reach *him*—I mean me, Blake—except straight. On the other hand, I might not believe you were only coming to get me. You might be headed for some other point—an installation of some sort maybe, way off to my right or left. But knowing you'd got Baksh I'd expect him to give away the fact that I was on this particular spot of the hills, and I'd not know whether you'd decide to avoid me or have a crack at me."

12 platoon commander said, "What does it matter, Tony? I've just cut off the bloke's head and I'm in a flat spin."

Ramsay said, "But is Blake? Will Blake be in a flat spin? What will Blake decide we're going to do? Let's assume that the Umpires will establish the situation for him on the lines we've discussed—that he gets no confirmation by air recce, no promise of help, only an order to increase patrol activity——"

Craig said, "You can count on that situation being established for him."

Ramsay nodded, said to the others, "Then where will Blake concentrate his patrol activity, knowing as he will that *we* know *he* knows we're in Khudabad."

They were silent until one of them said, "Anybody's guess. In other words, we ought to go ahead with what you'd originally planned."

Ramsay looked from one to the other, received their nods of agreement.

"Good. Then we're all of like mind. It's the conclusion I hoped we'd reach. At 0700 we'll evacuate this area and head for——" He gave a map reference. "We'll have another O group when we're re-formed, to study and plan for the march to the strongpoint."

"When shall we start for the strongpoint, Bob, today?"

"No. Today's a day of rest." He smiled. "There's one other thing. It isn't just anybody's guess where Blake's going to concentrate his patrol activity."

12 platoon commander said, "Does that mean you know."

"I mean we shall know."

"How? By recce patrols of our own?"

"No. He'll concentrate them where we want him to."

Ramsay looked at the Umpires. "At least, that's what we'll try to make him do."

When he got outside he realized that he was trembling, as though after physical exertion.

Craig (3)

THY SKY was quite overcast. Intermittently a hot wind blew through the open back of the truck, brought the dust with it. Ahead of them they could see the dust swirl up above the 30-cwt which led the way. The water wagon had dropped well behind.

They approached the road junction where Baksh had hitched his ride the day before. Thompson touched Craig's shoulder.

"Now we'll see."

Craig said, "No. There's nobody there." He told the driver to overtake the 30-cwt, turn left at the junction and then stop. When the driver had done this Craig looked back, past Thompson, who sat behind him. The 30-cwt, trailing its dust plume, continued along the road away from them, back towards the school. In due course the water wagon would follow it.

Thompson said, "There goes the konner."

Craig nodded. "Right. Now we'll visit Mr Blake."

At the second road junction they slowed down, but there was no lookout. They moved forward into the arms of the hills.

Blake, naked to the belt, moved his right hand again in its smoothing motion over belly and chest. Craig had a sense of power over him. He said, "No, they're keeping Baksh."

"I see, sir. I'm sorry. I didn't think, I suppose."

"It wasn't much in the spirit of the exercise, was it?"

"No. I do see that now, sir. But not at the time. I thought it was the right sort of move."

"Even after what I said about the importance of your not knowing where Ramforce is?"

Blake reddened.

Craig said, "Anyway, we'll forget it for the moment. But I want to make it clear that my umpiring report will disclose what happened, and as the school will send a copy of it to your CO you'd better take an early opportunity of owning up to him."

Blake grinned ruefully. He said, "I'll tell him about it. But need it go in the report? All sorts of brass hats'll see it, won't they?"

"Perhaps."

"It's up to you, sir, but if I——"

Craig broke in, "Don't misunderstand, Blake. The Baksh episode will feature in the report for one reason only, for the credit due to Ramsay for the way he dealt with it. It was Ramsay who discovered Baksh in the first place, and Ramsay who turned a fairly unscrupulous action into a scrupulously appreciated situation. If you'd been at his O group this morning you'd have seen what I meant. You *will* see what I mean because it's what I've come to tell you about."

An orderly pushed open the tent flap, moved carefully through it, so as not to spill the tea; he brought in two steaming mugs.

"What about your Sar-Major, sir?"

"I left him looking at your positions, but he'd like a cup, I expect."

Blake spoke to the orderly in fluent Urdu. Craig caught in him the look of pleasure he felt at having the opportunity to display at least one military virtue. He thought: He's not a bad chap, he tries hard.

And then: I like him for his faults, because he is ordinary, because his cunning is unconsidered, ham-fisted.

As he spoke of Ramsay he felt almost sorry for Blake. "This is the situation Ramsay has evolved. A few hours ago a man came in from, so he says, the village of Khudabad——"

Blake lowered his eyes over his tea.

"—with a message, so he says, from one Baksh, a villager who collaborates with you. The message is that the enemy have arrived in Khudabad in about company force and are believed to be headed in this direction. Baksh has been taken by them. The messenger says he saw this happen. He says Baksh was caught snooping around their lines and the last the messenger saw of him was under guard, going before the commanding officer for interrogation. Right?"

Blake grinned. "All right so far, sir."

"On receipt of this message you contacted your superior headquarters, who are presumed to be some distance removed from you, as you know. They didn't react very enthusiastically because they'd had many such rumours before during the year they've been stuck in this area. After a couple of hours they got on the blower to say that a light recce plane could see no sign of any such force in the Khudabad area. In fact, they go so far as to suggest that the messenger isn't telling the truth and is trying to attract a patrol in that direction, a patrol which will be ambushed by armed guerillas drawn from surrounding villages." Craig paused. "Right, Blake. Now you tell me what you'd do."

Blake looked nonplussed. He said, "But they *are* in Khudabad."

"How d'you know?"

"Because that's where your ration truck was going late yesterday afternoon."

"You're confusing one thing with another. But if we must talk about ration trucks, all you *know* is that the driver seemed to have instructions to go to Khudabad."

"Seemed to have? You mean it was a spoof?"

"I mean, Blake, that because yesterday one member of your

two-man lookout at that particular road junction came back to say that Havildar Baksh had thumbed a lift in the school ration truck which the driver said was going to Khudabad, I am developing for you now a situation in which you as the commander of a Japanese infantry company stationed here have received a report that the enemy are in Khudabad, and that report hasn't been confirmed by air reconnaissance."

"Oh, Lord! I mean—hell, what do I mean?"

"You mean that you're as confused as Ramsay wants you to be. Confused and very much on edge. So much on edge that you've beheaded the poor fellow who brought the message from Baksh. You applied torture, but the man insisted on telling the truth. You applied more torture. The man then doubled, trebled the reported number of enemy. That frightened you. You didn't want to hear any more, so you chopped him. You were afraid to bother superior headquarters again. All the help you got from them was an order to increase your patrol activities."

"In what direction?"

"They didn't say. They left it to you. You doubled your patrols, then got scared being so undermanned here. So you brought them all in. Have you got any patrols out at the moment, Blake?"

"No, sir. I usually send 'em out early morning and towards evening."

"Then the situation on the ground here is satisfactorily realistic at the moment."

Blake stood up. "Did young *Ramsay* think all this up?"

"You could put it that way."

"Then I'll look forward to meeting the young blighter."

"You will, Blake."

"When?"

Suddenly they grinned at each other.

Craig said, "That is a question that only Ramsay can answer."

For a while Craig let Blake wonder to himself, then he said, "Well?"

"I've worked it all out, sir. That young Ramsay *insured* against me keeping a lookout at the road junctions by briefing the driver to say he was going to Khudabad." He picked up his map. "When I got the word yesterday I thought it was a hell of a way to go. But if he's not in Khudabad, where the hell is he?"

"You tell me."

Blake had begun the smoothing motions with his hand again. He held the map out from his body and with his other hand rubbed his left breast muscle. His eyes met Craig's. "You want me to tell you what I think, sir?"

"It would be interesting."

"Nothing I say is divulged to Ramsay, is it?"

"I'm Chief Umpire, not a member of Ramforce. I should be glad if my cadets wiped the floor with you, but it would be just as good for them if you wiped the floor with them."

"Of course. Sorry, sir. Then this is what I think. I think he may be in this place Nanyaganj and plans to work his way along the river or even up the road. If that's right he could be here pretty soon. On the other hand the whole idea of the ration truck taking that road may be a complete spoof. There's this other road round the western slopes of the hills coming back round from Khudabad."

"Or there's Khudabad." Craig got up. "Blake. You're still looking at this all wrong. You're looking at it from the point of view of officer-cadet Ramsay conducting an exercise and dependent from time to time on ration trucks from the school. Can't you for once be what you're supposed to be and treat Ramsay as what he's supposed to be? Can't you accept the fact that you're here and he's somewhere you don't know? Reported at Khudabad, but unconfirmed?"

Blake put the map back on the table. "No, sir. Frankly I can't. I've been in the real thing."

"So have I. At least in what we call the real thing."

"Ramsay hasn't though, has he, sir? It may be real to him, but it can't ever be real to me. I know he's got me spoofed. But he's got me spoofed in terms of the exercise." He got out his cigarettes. Craig shook his head, watched Blake light one.

"Then all I'd ask you to remember, Blake, is that it's real to Ramsay. It's real to me, too."

Blake looked at him.

Craig explained. "What we're doing, the purpose of what we're doing, is real to me, that's what I mean. And there are certain things——" He hesitated. It was difficult to talk to Blake. "There are certain things which are real in any case."

The amused wariness which Craig had noticed at their first meeting had come back into Blake's face. He said rather abruptly. "What's the score about Havildar Baksh?"

"He's a prisoner."

Blake seemed to think about that, but his eyes never left Craig's. The feeling of power over Blake had gone and Craig was newly aware of the other man's stronger build and the smoothing motion of the hand became, now, a gentle, self-exploratory caress through which Blake subconsciously and mechanically gained courage from the muscular structure of his own body.

Blake had said, "What does being a prisoner involve in this case, sir?" and Craig now replied, "That you won't see him again."

"Until the end of the exercise."

"That's right."

"Does that mean he'll be forced to march with Ramsay?"

"Well, Blake, there's no alternative, is there?"

"I'd better send some rations back, if you'll take them, sir."

"We're on dry rations; he can share ours."

"He won't eat bully. I'll send him some tinned meat halal." Blake paused, as if deliberately. "And his uniform."

"He won't need that. He's more conspicuous in white civvies. We can keep an eye on him better."

"Then I'll send his boots."

When, with Thompson, Craig had inspected the positions Blake had laid down in an area commanding the road with outposts on the centre ridge, he returned to the scarred slope where woodcutters had once worked and where Blake had pitched his tent.

The wind was turning the leaves upwards. The lighter green showed silvery against the blackening sky. It was a hot wind, like oven-blast. It stirred the forest and they had to raise their voices against its spasmodic, angry gusts.

"You know I'm leaving Sar-Major Thompson to umpire your side of things?"

"Yes, sir."

"He's brought his rations."

"And I've put Baksh's in your truck, sir."

Craig turned to Thompson. "Have a good time, Sar-Major."

"Thank you, sir. Don't keep us waiting too long."

"I'll see that Ramsay gets your message. Well, thank you, Blake. I'll see you again in due course. Keep your patrols working, won't you? Don't forget that it's part of Ramsay's task to *avoid* being bumped by patrols."

"Right, sir."

Blake followed him to the truck. The driver stood in the open with a few of Blake's men who, on Blake's approach, withdrew.

Craig grinned at Blake. "If they've been trying to pump my driver they won't have had any joy. He was well briefed."

"I'm sure he was, sir."

"Tell my Sar-Major I'll be putting this truck at his disposal. He can expect it to reach him here sometime tomorrow morning."

"Right. You won't forget Baksh's boots and rations, will you, sir? They're in the back."

"I won't forget."

As Craig got into the truck the wind began to suck dust devils out of the road. Head bent against it, he saw Blake shield his eyes with an arm. The devils spun like tumblers, away up the road. The bonnet of the truck was scarcely visible through the windscreen. Slowly Blake straightened up and as he did so the first blare of thunder rumbled up from behind the centre ridge, and when it had gone the wind dropped and in the silence Craig and Blake looked at each other.

"Goodbye then, Blake."

"Goodbye, sir."

The driver had wiped the windscreen over, now returned to the wheel and pressed the starter. A raindrop, two inches in diameter, appeared on the bonnet. Craig fixed his eyes on it as the truck began to move, back along the way it had come. Another blob appeared on the bonnet, but the rain held off until they had passed the junction where the western track joined the road they were on. It came, then, turned the wind-screen into an opaque, liquid rectangle, through which they could see only a distorted, marooned landscape.

They turned off to the right at the next junction where yesterday Baksh had waited, faced now squarer to the storm. In the south-western sky the lightning etched itself sharp, blue-white and jagged. By the time they reached the bridge below Nanyaganj the dry top surface of the dust road had already washed away and the water had begun to eat into the caked earth below.

On the bridge Craig told the driver to stop. He stared down at the river. He could have sworn that the channel of water had perceptibly widened and its forward movement strengthened. The surface of the water was alive, pitted and galvanized by the downpour, and to Craig it seemed that this life came to it from underneath, was forced to the surface by a violent agitation of the river bed itself. And here, on the bridge, he heard the voice of the river above the voice of the storm.

It was dark when they reached Khudabad. The engine of the truck had been knocking for some time and their arrival was, for Craig—exhausted from sharing the anxiety the driver expressed only in silence—a small, mechanical victory.

With nightfall the rain had stopped and the air was chill. A man, raincape slung back behind his shoulders, came into their headlights. The driver, speaking at last, said happily, "Sergeant Shaw, sahib," slowed, braked, kept the engine running.

Shaw bent to the cabin. "Evening, sir. Nice weather for the ducks."

"Hello, Staff."

"There's a place down the road in the village where you can get the truck under cover, sir. Ramsay's runner's with me. We've got a brew on."

"Good show, Staff. Lead us in, will you?"

Shaw trotted ahead, for there was no running-board on the 8-cwt. Directed by him they turned into the main road of the village and drove to the end of it. A light showed from one of the empty huts and a figure darkened the doorway. Shaw, in their headlights, walked backwards, guided them round into a byrelike structure which was roofed but open on the side which faced east. The hut where the runner stood was adjacent.

In the hut the four of them drank scalding tea. The thunder rumbled again and Shaw said, "The boys have got hold of an idea about the village, sir."

"Tell me."

"They say there must be a man-eater in the forest."

"A tiger?"

The runner grinned, embarrassed but amused. "Yes, sir. The idea is that the tiger hides up in the forest and pops down every other day to eat a villager. So they cleared out."

"And the tiger went too?"

"No, sir. He's still there. Or she. Probably an old female tiger with a festering wound."

Craig smiled, said, "It's not an unreasonable conjecture."

Shaw said, "Except we'd have heard about it at the school. It'd 've been big news for miles around when it happened."

The runner said, "It was a private tiger, Staff." He looked at Craig. "The story began when some of us were talking to Baksh, sir."

"And was he suitably impressed?"

"Don't know, sir. He looked a bit thoughtful, even though he laughed it off."

Craig said, "I've got special rations for him in the truck. His Lieutenant sent them. Baksh seems to be a strict Muslim and won't eat bully, so they've sent him some tinned meat halal. D'you know what halal is?"

"Yes, sir. Where you slit its throat."

"What is Hindu meat?"

"Jhatka, sir. Where you chop its head off."

"I see you've learned something."

Shaw said, "Are you going up to see them tonight, sir?"

"No . . . I'll sleep here tonight." He turned back to the runner. "Tell Ramsay, will you? I'll come out first thing tomorrow morning. What time d'you start?"

"0800, sir."

"Right." He gave Shaw his map. "Mark up for me just where they are, Staff, will you?"

"I can lead you there in the morning, sir."

"No. I want you to go back now. If I'm not with you by 0700 send back to check with me, will you? I'm sending the truck back for the Sar-Major's use, so I want to see it safely on its way. It gave some trouble tonight."

Shaw marked the map and gave it back to him. "It's just over a mile, sir. The going's not too bad."

"You both be getting along, then. Have you got anything to carry Baksh's stuff in?"

"Depends how much there is, sir."

"It's in the back of the truck. His boots are there, too."

Shaw hesitated. "Right, sir. And his boots."

Shaw went out with the runner. When they returned Shaw had the boots slung by their laces round his neck. The runner carried the tins of meat. He put two into the large thigh pocket of his trousers and began to stuff more down his shirt-front.

Shaw said, "What's he preparing for, a siege? Here, give some to me."

When they were ready Craig said, "Give Baksh's stuff to Ramsay, not to Baksh."

Shaw said, "I wondered," and grinned at the runner. "Come on."

The runner said, "Good night, sir."

"Don't get lost."

Shaw, over his shoulder, said, "Or eaten by the tiger. 'Night, sir."

He heard them laugh aloud in the street. He went out, watched them go, heard them for a while after the darkness had covered them. In the byre the driver was bent over the exposed engine of the truck, a hurricane lantern slung from a beam in the roof.

Craig said, in Urdu, "What is the trouble, brother?"

The driver straightened, smiled. "In the petrol pump there is water, sahib. Too much water."

"That will not be difficult to make right?"

"After a little while it will give no trouble, sahib."

"Good. Did the soldiers ask you many questions?"

"Too many questions, sahib."

"How did you answer them?"

"That I was a simple man and did not understand." He grinned. "When they asked me whether we were in Khudabad I said to them, yes, we were all in the abode of God, that they also were in this place, because the abode of God is everywhere, even in the forest."

"What did they say then?"

"They were laughing, sahib, and they gave me some chappatties and some rice. I have put these in my mess-tin and when I have made the engine all right I will eat well."

"Good. Now I also will eat."

"You would like some rice and chappatties, sahib?"

"No, thank you, my brother. What I have for myself, I will eat."

Later, when he had eaten bully and dry biscuit, he heard the man singing softly to himself in the byre. He made his bed in a corner of the hut, turned out the lantern and watched the night take shape through the open door. It took the shape of the song that the man sang and entered with him into the dream.

Now when he had fought through the forest and come to the wide, burning plain, he was not alone. At his side walked Esther and the song returned in snatches and when it no longer returned it seemed that he had gone out of the dream with the song and that the dream of Esther was a dream which dreamed itself and that he reached out to draw it into himself as Esther walked across the plain, or stood at a doorway, in all the guises of love.

And Esther moved through the dream, displayed through gesture and voice, which was not voice but idea of voice, her ignorance of his being no longer beside her. Do not be so alone, Esther, he called, and as she went down the hill he felt his love move out and touch the space around her, and the runner was there, and Blake, and Sergeant Shaw, and the driver in the dark byre, and he called out to them once before he turned and walked to the place where Baksh waited to take him to Ramsay.

Craig (4)

WHEN THE truck had gone he was alone in Khudabad. The rain was falling, but there was no wind. The land lay opne to the grey morning sky and the only sounds were the diminishing sound of the departed truck and the steady unbroken sound of the falling rain.

As he fastened the straps of his pack and settled it on his shoulders he remembered the dream and going to the doorway beyond which the rain waited to receive him he thought: That was the end of the dream, the dream has gone out of me, I am alone in Khudabad and Ramsay is alone in the forest. When I enter the forest today I shall be the hunter, he the quarry.

He left the doorway and the rain soaked him through in a few seconds. He carried in his mind a picture of the shapes and colours of the map but for a moment, as he screwed his eyes against the rain, the ground ahead of him would not fit the picture in his mind and he stood still, lost. And then he said to himself: But it must fit, because I have given my life purpose. I create Ramsay in the image of the man I should have been perhaps, but could not be: the image of a man who feels the need to destroy his enemies, who finds this need greater than his own need to live, who therefore mocks his life.

Almost without knowing Craig moved towards the forest. I'm wrong, he thought, I do not create Ramsay in this image. It is the image in which he is cast and I take his hand and move the fingers across his brow so that he may feel grown there indelibly into the flesh the stamp, the mark of the warrior, and when he has felt this mark and understood its nature he will be a man into whose hands the rest of us may place our lives.

John said: Finish me off: but I did not finish him off because while he lived there was hope for us of the forest and when he died there were left ourselves and death, and only luck dividing us from it, or mercy, divine providence, what you will. A man could not trust in luck, or in mercy. In the forest he could trust only in the destroyed man, the man who beat and hammered and shaped the senses of living men into a single weapon to demonstrate his will and knowledge of the enemy. Ramsay must prove to be such a man.

Ramsay turned when Craig reached the top of the slope where he stood alone with a view beyond the trees of the scrub-strewn valley which lay between them and the next jungle-clad hill.

Ramsay looked at his watch. "You're early, sir. Have you had breakfast?"

"Yes, thank you, Ramsay. How soon d'you move off?"

"Not until 0800. More than an hour."

"What sort of night did you have?"

"Fair, sir. The rain kept off until four."

"I know. The storm woke me. Let's go down to that shelter you've rigged up for HQ. I want to hear your plans of march."

"Right, sir."

Craig led the way down the hill, past one of the perimeter-guard who was soaked but cheerful, cape-clad on a ledge which jutted above and gave a view of about fifty yards down a ravine.

Lawson was alone in the shelter. He said to Craig, "Havildar Baksh wants to see you, sir."

The three of them stood in the shelter, heads bowed beneath the low roof. Craig said, "I'm Chief Umpire, Lawson. I don't exist for Baksh. I only exist for Ramsay. Baksh may see Ramsay if Ramsay wishes." After a moment he added, "Shall you see Baksh?"

"Afterwards, sir. You want to know the plan of march."

"Yes."

The canvas of Ramsay's map-case was sodden. When the flap was unbuttoned the protective mica window beneath which the map lay had to be mopped with his handkerchief. He passed the open case to Craig and gave him a reference number.

"Is that the strongpoint?"

"Yes, sir."

"Well?"

"We march there by the direct route."

"Up the hills and down the hills."

"Yes. We go as far as we can today, the rest tomorrow. We'll move through the jungle by platoons spaced out in single file. Between platoons there'll be contact men. The contact man in the rear of a platoon will be responsible for keeping in touch with the man at the head of the following platoon. If he loses touch he sends up the word to halt."

"What about the mules?"

"They'll be behind 11 and 12 platoons, but in front of 10."

"10 platoon goes in the rear this time?"

"Yes, sir. I'm putting 12 platoon up front."

"What about yourself?"

"I shall go at the head of 12 platoon."

"You're the pathfinder."

"Yes, sir. I'll take my runner. Lawson will take the command group and go at the rear of 12 platoon."

"What about flank protection?"

"None, sir."

"Why?"

"It would slow us up to put men on the flank of the column. I'm aiming at the sharpest forward movement possible."

"How would you cope with an ambush, or an enemy patrol bumping your flank?"

"As best we could. But I don't expect enemy patrols farther south of the river than the strongpoint. In fact I hardly expect them south of the river at all. The river must be filling up. If they had men dug in on Elephant Hill they'll either withdraw north of the river or remain there virtually cut off."

"You make the rain your ally?"

Ramsay said, "Yes. I wanted the rain. I waited for the rain."

Craig nodded, said, "But can you count on having the forest to yourself? Supposing that on the first day Blake had sent a patrol in force south of the river? As you say, they might now be cut off, but they might be there. Suppose they are there?"

"I've thought of that. The risk is a small one. If I broaden the front of our approach by putting out flank protection I'd increase the odds of bumping them."

"That's true, Ramsay. But even if they didn't see you they would probably hear you. They'd probably hear a column of one hundred men and a mule train cutting its way through the jungle."

"I've minimized that risk. There'll be no talking on the march other than what is essential for passing orders. Mule harness is being muffled with sacking. And the rain's our ally there as well. That's why you found me up on the hill by myself. I wanted to hear the sound of the rain and to what extent it muffled the sound of the camp."

They fell silent, stranded in a dark green world of falling rain, and it seemed to Craig that a man lost there, hurt there, might call and call and not be heard. He thought of the time, one year ago, when he had moved through such a world and been afraid because the sound of the rain might deaden the sound of the enemy, because in a world empty of all sound but the sound of the rain the enemy might come and kill and go in silence. Here now was Ramsay stranded with him in such a world, and the fear was not there because Ramsay saw and heard and communicated to those around him a different world, in which the enemy were mute and blind and deaf and beyond reaching them.

Ramsay said to Lawson, "We'd better see what Baksh wants," and Lawson went to the opening of the shelter and raised his voice against the rain. Baksh must have been waiting ready, because he came almost at once. His *dhoti* and cotton shirt, streaked with dirt, clung to his body. He came to attention at the entrance.

Ramsay said, "Come in, Havildar."

Craig said, when he had joined them, "Mr Lawson said you wanted to see me. I'm afraid my duties are confined to those of umpiring, but I can listen to what you have to say to Mr Ramsay."

In Urdu Baksh replied, "But it is a personal matter, sahib."

Craig said, in English, "We must talk in English if we can. Tell us what the matter is and I will decide whether it is personal between you and me."

"They are telling, sir, that Lieutenant Blake Sahib is sending something to me yesterday."

"That is a matter for Mr Ramsay and not for me. Ramsay?"

Ramsay said, "You say they are telling. Who are they?"

"The muleteer, sahib. All yesterday the muleteer is good friend to me and shares his rations——"

Craig interrupted. "The muleteer can afford to be a good friend, Havildar. He is not a cadet and has his full rations. The cadets are on half rations."

"This I know, sir. Yesterday he said, 'Today you will share with me. The Major Sahib has gone to your Lieutenant Sahib and when he returns he will bring your rations.' So also say all the cadet-sahibs who show much friendship and joking to me, sir. This morning the muleteer is saying that the cadet-sahibs speak both of rations and boots which Sergeant Shaw Sahib bring into camp last night. To this time I have not received them and the muleteer again giving me food, but not willingly, knowing that my own rations are brought."

Craig said, "What the muleteer says is true, Havildar. Lieutenant Blake Sahib sent both rations and boots. Sergeant Shaw Sahib brought them to Mr Ramsay last night on my instructions. It is for Mr Ramsay to decide what should be done with them. You are his prisoner. You mustn't forget that, Havildar."

Ramsay said, "You'll find them wrapped in that groundsheet in the corner."

Baksh looked down where Ramsay pointed.

"Go on. You can have them."

The man moved to the corner, knelt, unwrapped the groundsheet. He held the boots up, inspected them, put them down, seemed to count the tins. Then he stood up, left the things where they were.

Craig said, "What's the matter?"

"Lieutenant Blake Sahib sent no pack, sir?"

"No. He forgot to send a pack."

"Or socks, sir?"

Craig stared down at the boots. "He forgot socks."

Baksh knelt again. "This is not my groundsheet, sahib."

Lawson said, "No, it's mine."

Baksh was silent. Then he unbuttoned his long cotton shirt, stripped it off. He laid out the shirt on the ground, counted the tins, placed half the tins on the shirt and tied it into a bundle.

Ramsay said, "You've left half the tins."

"They are too much to carry. Too many rations for one man." Baksh stood up.

Ramsay said, "Aren't you going to take the boots?"

"I cannot wear boots without socks, sir. I am not African askari or barefoot peasant."

"What about the rest of the tins?"

"What I have is enough, sir."

Ramsay asked, "And who carries the boots and the rest of your rations?"

"I will put the boots round my neck. Perhaps the rations can be left. Perhaps the mules——"

"The mules have a full load. And we can't leave rations abandoned in the jungle. In terms of the exercise neither the rations nor the boots exist, but since your Lieutenant Sahib saw fit to send them we'll have to call for one or two volunteers to help you carry them."

Baksh, about to reply, hesitated, then threw the bundle on to the floor. He spoke to Craig, in Urdu. "The cadet-sahib brings much dishonour to me. I obey the orders of Lieutenant Blake Sahib, I am taken prisoner. I have no food, no boots, no blanket, no groundsheet. The cadet-sahib says that I must march two, three days, through the forest. Have I done wrong that I should suffer? If I must march must I not eat also? Must I beg each mouthful from men who are themselves hungry and feel anger with me because my hunger adds to their hunger? If I cannot carry all that my Lieutenant Sahib, who loves me, sends me, must other men be made to carry also?"

Craig said to Ramsay, "Did you understand?"

"Yes."

In English Craig said, "You must realize, Havildar Baksh, that Mr Ramsay is not a cadet but the commander of Ramforce, and that you are not a Havildar in Mr Blake's company but a villager who spies for the Japanese. Mr Ramsay's attitude to you is not a personal one and you mustn't blame him.

Perhaps you should blame me. I think I was wrong to accept what Mr Blake gave me. I don't know. It was difficult." He found himself looking to Ramsay. His mind could not shut out the picture of Baksh as Baksh, of the boots and the rations as what they were, of Baksh's need of them, and he could not conjure the picture that these made for Ramsay.

He said to Baksh and Lawson, "Mr Ramsay and I had better talk about this together. We'll call you back when we've reached a decision."

Alone with Ramsay he said, "We must kill Baksh."

"Why?"

"We can't do otherwise. Look. I'll develop a situation for you here and now. You've interrogated Baksh, he's told you nothing. You can't drag him through the forest, so as he's dangerous alive you shoot him. Baksh is finished with for you. He's now an umpiring problem. He comes with me. He takes what rations he can. We'll leave the rest here or I'll put them in my pack. He can have my spare socks. He can have what I like to give him because he's nothing more to do with you, Ramsay, he's only got to do with me. He and I are not in the picture, not in your picture as commander of Ramforce."

"I can't accept that, sir," Ramsay said.

"Why not?"

"I need Baksh as a prisoner."

"He's only an embarrassment to you, Ramsay. What earthly good is he as a prisoner?"

Ramsay took out his cigarettes, found them sodden, useless, put them back in his pocket. He said, "Baksh is here because Blake cheated. I intend to turn Baksh into a rope Blake's made to hang himself." He had lowered his voice and Craig went closer in order to hear, as though they were conspirators in the matter of Baksh.

Ramsay went on, "I'm supposing that Baksh the villager has told us little of value, but has admitted that through him the enemy now know we're in the forest. He's told us roughly where the enemy are disposed. What he doesn't bargain for is to be taken through the forest with us, but that's what we do, and when he realizes that we're only an isolated group and not the spearhead of an army, he regrets having co-operated with us, because he knows we'll go in and come out and leave him still in occupied territory. He decides to pretend to be friendly to discover all he can about our plans and then, when he's near the enemy, escape and tip them off."

Craig said, "As commander of this force you'd be unlikely to fall for his friendliness. It you take him with you in the hope that nearer the time, under new threats, he'll tell you more, then you'll have him under the closest observation and give him no chance to escape."

"I agree. But we could let him escape with the wrong information."

"What wrong information?"

"When we get to the strongpoint we'll prepare for a march to the river-crossing at the ford five miles *west* of the crossing below Elephant Hill. We'll do more than prepare for it. We'll send the column off in that direction and leave only a token force at the strongpoint. Baksh will be allowed to escape from the strongpoint. He'll cross the river below Elephant Hill and go straight to Blake, who'll send a force to contest our supposed crossing at the ford. Meanwhile our own force will have doubled back. We'll cross at Elephant Hill, occupy Blake's positions and destroy his detached force by a march on his rear." Ramsay paused. "That's what I meant at yesterday's orders group about Blake concentrating his patrol activity where we wanted him to concentrate it."

"I see."

Ramsay said, "You have reservations?"

"Yes. Baksh might suspect he's being allowed to escape, or even not bother or want to escape."

"Let's take the first. Baksh might suspect. He might. It's a risk, so I have to minimize it. First, he mustn't appear to be told where the crossing's going to be. I've thought about that and decided that Lawson, who'll be left in charge of the strongpoint, won't be told to allow Baksh to escape until we're actually starting off for the feinted crossing. And I'll have relied on Baksh learning where we're off to from general camp talk. No one'll be told not to tell him and no one'll be told to tell him. He'll learn about it in the way he learned about the boots and the rations. Up until the moment I tell Lawson to let him escape only you and I'll know that we're not marching all the way to the five-mile ford and crossing there."

"How far will you go?"

"A mile or two. An hour's march. Then we'll stop and wait until Lawson sends back a message that Baksh has gone and at what time. Baksh'll probably wait for quite a while before deciding we really have gone. If he hasn't gone by a certain hour Lawson will send a message to that effect and then he'll not be allowing Baksh to escape, and we'll carry on and cross at the five-mile ford."

"Yes. That's sensible. But you'd prefer Baksh to fall for it and escape."

"Yes. I think he will fall for it and I think he'll escape. There are two reasons why he'll escape and one reason why he may not. He'll escape if he's feeling loyal to Blake and entering into the spirit of the exercise Blake's inculcated in him—or he'll escape if he's unhappy with us. He may not escape if he's having a cushy time, dead for the purposes of the exercise."

Craig said, "So Baksh must be unhappy with us?"

"As a prisoner he would be unhappy, and afraid. It wouldn't matter if the prisoner didn't have a part in my plan. Baksh could then be as happy as a lark for all I cared. But I need the prisoner. I need the idea of the prisoner. It's a role Baksh has got to perform. He won't perform it if he has to imagine everything." He broke off, then said with a kind of anger. "I can't do all their imagining for them."

"Then let's decide on the source of Baksh's unhappiness. What do you do? Make him carry everything himself in his shirt and wear boots without socks?"

After a moment Ramsay said, "Surely that would make him a martyr? He'd enjoy that and the others'd be sorry for him once they'd stopped laughing at the sight he made."

Craig said, Ramsay's contempt twisting in him like a blade, "You're becoming something of a psychologist," and then his knowledge that Ramsay was right twisted the blade farther, deeper, until the soft core of his own understanding of men was pierced and he stood a hunter wounded by the thing he hunted. Defenceless, he gestured, invited the despatch.

"So what do you do with Baksh?"

"I shall call the platoon commanders and tell them the truth, that Blake has seen fit to burden his havildar with these things and that Baksh is only willing to carry what he wants to carry. I'll ask them to call for volunteers to carry Baksh's rations and another volunteer to give up a spare pair of socks."

"And so?"

"Divided up, the actual weight is nothing. There'll be plenty of volunteers. After two days' march through the jungle, with Baksh walking unencumbered, on full rations which he doesn't carry, and in a spare pair of socks the man who's given them will probably need, he won't be so popular. Even if the men accept it philosophically, Baksh'll feel—as he puts it—dishonoured. In other words, he'll be in much the same state of mind towards us as Baksh the villager would be. And we'll be in something of the state of mind towards him that we'd be towards the prisoner." Ramsay smiled. "And Baksh'll keep the idea of Blake as a bastard nicely alive."

Craig said presently, "Baksh the villager would have neither boots nor rations."

"I was ready to deal with it in this way, but Baksh has refused. Blake gave them to you, sir, and you brought them. If you say they don't now exist, I'll have to accept that and lay on that he begs rations from us and walks in sandals or barefoot."

Craig said, "The others might be sorry for him, then. Don't you think that, Ramsay? That the general feeling would be that it wasn't his fault and that he was having a raw deal? You might be surprised at how comfortable they'd make him if they were sorry for him."

"No. I wouldn't be surprised. That was the thing that worried me before you brought the stuff Blake sent. At first, when I decided Baksh would have to have it rough, I was only thinking of it in terms of Baksh, of his having it rough and wanting to escape."

"When did you first think of having him escape?"

"Just before the orders group yesterday morning. But during the day when I saw that he was becoming a sort of mascot I realized I'd have to think of Baksh in terms of the others, and the effect his having it rough would have on them."

Craig said, "What were you going to do about it?"

"I didn't know. It was the real blow Blake struck, only he wouldn't realize it. But he gave us a means of warding it off when he sent the boots and rations."

"Were you going to give Baksh the boots and rations?"

"Yes, because then he'd have it cushy in relation to the other men. But I wanted him to get bolshie first."

"How did you know he'd get bolshie?"

"I should have said it stands out a mile. He's the type. Hail-fellow-well-met when there's something to be got out of it like the muleteer's rations, but a bastard if he suspects some-one's putting it over on him."

"Then why did you want him to get bolshie?"

"To wipe out as much of the hail-fellow-well-met flavour as possible. He's done that quite effectively. He's shouted the odds over his boots and rations and having got 'em he won't carry more than he finds comfortable."

"I think he could be made to."

"I don't want him to be made to, sir. He's shouted the odds. All right. We carry them for him. He's cooked his goose and the men are going to be pretty browned off with him, particu-larly as from now on he'll sulk like a small boy."

Craig stared at him. He said, "Ramsay, why do you want the men to dislike Baksh?"

Ramsay stared back, surprise growing on his face. "But he's the villager, sir. They wouldn't like a man who's tipped off the enemy about them."

Now Craig saw that Ramsay had truly crossed the barrier which separated the one reality from the other. He said, "All right—call your platoon commanders. Call Baksh," and it seemed to him that, as he said the words, he delivered himself with the others into the hands of the whole man who was not for them a man at all but the sum of their separate longing to survive in the dark, green, drowned world.

Ramsay (4)

THE CENTRE of the strongpoint lay in a deep scrub-grown hollow between the converging spurs of parallel ridges, and they reached it on the evening of the second day. As on the first evening of the march, the rain had died as though weary of itself, the sun shone briefly, low to the rim of the hills, and the foliage steamed, gave off its smell of green decay, dried and warmed the flesh where it was exposed, so that beneath wet clothing the covered flesh felt cold.

He stood where he could watch the column appear, man by man, out of the dark jungle. He had come on alone, except for his runner, from the last halt, and now as the others encroached he felt himself extended, his soaked and beaten body stretched, racked, as one by one, with their approach, they laid claim again to their need of him.

The head of the first platoon faltered as if his presence, his immobility, laid on them an obligation to halt. He urged them on towards and past him by repeated jerks of both thumbs over his shoulders, shouted to 12 platoon commander, "Get 'em up on the ridge," and Angus yelled, "Up the hill, chaps, up the bloody hill." He stopped by Ramsay, said, "Dig in on the ridge?"

"As best you can. We're here for twenty-four hours. I'll have 11 platoon on your left. Fix y'r boundary with Paddy. Tony'll be down here with me and the mules."

"I heard the mules'd dropped behind again."

"— the bloody mules."

"Not my line. When's prayers?"

"I'll send word. Get a brew on."

12 platoon commander went up the ridge. As 11 platoon commander passed him Ramsay said, "Up the hill, Paddy. Left of Angus. Get a brew on."

The cadet stopped, nodded dumbly. Yellow-white muck rimmed his lips.

Ramsay said, "Have you kept contact with the mule train?"

The cadet shook his head and then, as if prodded, jerked forward. Ramsay turned to his runner. "Go back and see how far behind the mules are and if Tony's waiting for 'em."

"OK, Bob." The runner began at a mechanical trot, stumbled, limped back into the jungle.

In Ramsay's body was an understanding that if he sat down he would not stand up again. He stood. There was no feeling in his feet, only a sensation of weight. The muscles of his legs and thighs trembled, but the trembling was like the vibration in metal. His hands and arms were dead, long since atrophied by the weight of the pack from which it seemed they were now mere protuberances like thick fleshy straps which, oddly, could be galvanized in the way of hands and arms. He told himself: If I take the pack off I shall never put it on again. If I take the pack off I shall lose my arms, my hands.

He rested his dead right hand on his revolver holster and the blood tingled in it until it hurt.

For a long time he stared at the opening into the jungle from which the men had ceased to erupt. His extended body was now poised uncertainly, deprived of the final eruption which would give it wholeness, complete identity, and in this state of half-being his mind rebelled and he wished that the jungle would close on the one side and on the other to swallow both the men who had not come and the men who had come and now moved invisibly upon the ridge to lay upon it part of the pattern of safety he had devised.

I am safe, he thought; in myself, by myself, there is safety. I could go now, alone, or stay here, alone. I am in myself all that I want of myself, and the safety I have devised is not for myself but for a force which represents me. The patterns which I lay down on the ground in the forms of men are the patterns of my own body which can both attack and defend. Here, where I stand, is the heart of the pattern. Here, where I stand, I stand, and for some reason it is not enough.

It is not enough because the thing that I hunt, the thing which waits and defends itself against me is not a man but a pattern devised by a man which describes that man. I am not a man who moves through the forest to attack this other man. I have become a pattern which moves through the forest to attack another pattern, and in the struggle between pattern and pattern is the shape of the struggle between myself and this other man; between myself and Blake. Blake and I fight each other in patterns. My right arm is a platoon of men which moves over the ground as my arm might move through the air to strike. My doubled fist is a spearhead of men and the weapons they carry are the knife I might grip in that fist.

The sun was below the hill now and he stood in shadow and watched the place in the jungle where the men who would complete his pattern must emerge. He stared for so long without moving his eyes from one spot that they began to play with him the jungle tricks with which he had become familiar. The trunk of a tree half exposed behind the laced creepers and leaves and branches was a man, silent, watchful. The movement created by a current of air was the movement which followed the bending, the sharp twisting of a body. The leaf which trembled from the fall of a drop of water from the leaf above, trembled from the touch of a finger.

It is not a man, he told himself, it is not the movement of a body, or the touch of a finger. It is a man and a movement and a finger only to men who have no forest-wisdom and are incapable of becoming a pattern, who are not extended, stretched through the forest. From where I wait I have knowledge of the ridge behind me that I have not myself trodden, and of the part of the forest where my eyes saw movement and from which part of me has yet to emerge. The men on the ridge and the men who are still in the jungle do not have this knowledge because they are only the nerves reaching into the centre. I am the centre reaching out through the medium of the nerves.

But this centre and this nerve pattern is not myself. It is what I am forced to be, but wish not to be. I would wish to sever the nerves from the centre and let the centre go back into myself so that I might be alone in the forest and move in my own safety towards an end or a beginning of my own making.

It would be easy, he thought, to turn now and go into the forest alone in the gathering darkness. But he continued to stand, motionless, and in a while he heard the sounds that the stragglers made as they came down the spur.

A new storm raged in the night, but in the morning the sky broke clear of cloud and the sun swam out of the mist and burnt the moisture away. The men moved half naked through the scrub to get the heat on their backs and the spring back into their limbs.

At 0800 a patrol moved north to see what could be found on Elephant Hill and another patrol moved north-west to reconnoitre the route to the ford five miles upstream of the hill. In the forest the thud of machete and axe echoed around the hollow.

The sun was a good omen. It blessed their enterprise. Ramsay stood bareheaded, bare-chested to it, eyes half closed, and drank in the smell of the land. He moved on through the scrub, spoke to the muleteer, ignored the deliberately averted gaze of Baksh who squatted, tailor-fashion, beneath a thorn under the eye of a guard.

The guard jerked his head towards the sound of the chopping, said, "What are we making, Bob?"

And Ramsay slapped the neck of the mule he stood by and answered, "A raft."

He moved up the slope into the gloom of the interlaced trees. A group of men sang rhythmically away to his right. While there was the necessity of chopping, he thought, they might as well sing. They could sing the silence out of themselves, and the doubt and discouragement which the discipline of silence fostered. He stood where he could not be seen and closed his eyes again and felt the pattern of the ridge and the hollow grow into him. Lines of sensitivity now probed outwards from the centre towards Elephant Hill and towards the five-mile ford, and the centre was protected by patrolling guards around the perimeter.

When he had finished his inspection of the ridge and of the preliminary work on the raft-building he descended to the hollow and to the fierce sun and to a sense of invulnerability which was compounded of joy in the sun and confidence in the pattern. He would move the pattern through the forest to the river, over the river, and superimpose it over Blake's pattern. He would do this.

The Elephant Hill patrol returned after the midday meal in high spirits. He listened to their report, sent them away to eat. The sun was overhead, stabbed directly into the hollow. An hour later, sweat-stained, pushed to the limit, the ford patrol came in. At 1500 hours he called a company assembly. It was, he knew, time for a gesture which defied the discipline he had enforced, a gesture which emphasized their invulnerability, which brought them together as at a picnic.

Leaving the skeleton patrols on the perimeter and a guard on Baksh and the mules, men clambered from the hill, through the scrub, converged on Ramsay where he stood, fully uniformed and armed, in an open patch of ground where they had room to squat shoulder to shoulder, eyes raised to him. Craig leaned against the trunk of a tree, was joined by Shaw.

When they had all quietened Ramsay paused deliberately, then said, "With any luck we should end this scheme tomorrow morning." The cheer which followed made him smile. He said, "Unless the umpires direct otherwise." They groaned, good-humouredly, looked to Craig, back to Ramsay. Now, as they waited, at ease, friendly, he wondered why he could not feel himself one of them. That was gone for ever. He had been one of them once, briefly. He had not been so for a long time. He did not know why, suddenly, the thought should take shape that he could not feel himself bound by the ties by which they were bound.

He said, "From what our patrols say we needn't expect Blake's crowd to bust in on us, so I thought we'd save time, have a general O group and enjoy the sun while it lasts.

"As you know, we sent out two patrols this morning. One to recce the feature known as Elephant Hill and the river below it, and one to recce a route to another part of the river where there's a ford. The reason for the double patrol was twofold. First, to recce as much of the area in front of us as possible in case Blake had some surprise in store for us this side of the river. Second, to decide which point of the river to make our crossing.

"The patrol commanders have probably talked about what

they found, so it may not be news to you. But let's hear from them now."

He looked into the crowd for the patrol leaders. They stood up and came out to the front.

"Elephant Hill first."

The cadet stood near Ramsay and described what he had seen. "First of all you'll be glad to know that the jungle between here and the river isn't anything like as bad as what we've come through. We made good time and found a track down in the ravine the other side of the ridge we're dug in on. Eventually the track took us to the bottom of the southern face of Elephant Hill. When we got there we thought we'd do a bit of a detour, so we went east a bit and went up the south-east slope."

Someone shouted, "Crafty bastards."

The cadet grinned and said, "Belt up that man. Anyway, we went up the south-east slope, pretty cautious because Bob said there might be a listening post or something at the top. As a matter of fact there was. We heard 'em moving about from about fifty yards. There were six sepoys and a naik, and pretty browned off they looked when we caught sight of them."

"Browned off at the sight of you, Bill."

"They didn't see us. We stalked them down the hill to the river. They were pulling out—going back across—and we reckon Blake'd told 'em to get back before the river got any higher. It's about waist deep where we saw them cross, but the flow's pretty fast and one of 'em came a cropper in the middle. Anyway, they pulled out. We waited around in case a relief section came over, but nothing happened for about half an hour, then a chap we think was Blake appeared on the opposite bank with a havildar and they sort of stared at the river a bit, then buggered off. So we thought we'd do the same."

The cadet sat down. In the back of the crowd there was a round of applause. The cadet grinned over his shoulder at them and waggled two fingers in the air. The leader of the ford patrol took his place at the front and waited for their attention.

"By comparison with Bill's patrol ours was rather dull, but I bear him out about the going. We went down the ridge into the ravine where it's just scrub jungle, and we reckoned that if the chap who drew the map had got his contours right we could use the ravine to take us to within a mile of the ford. I'm glad to say he gets full marks for his contours. The only really rough going is when you get to the head of the ravine and have to climb out of it up on to a ridge and then down the other side, but that brings you out on to a road track that takes you straight to the ford, only it's not a very good ford. I mean, you get pretty wet if you want to reach the other side. Bill said the river's waist deep at his crossing. At our ford it came up to about thigh level. Three of us went over to test it. It runs quite fast and I'd say it's rising and has quite a way to go before it's full. We didn't bump any of Blake's men and we don't think we were seen. By that I mean we didn't get the feeling of being watched."

Ramsay looked at him with deeper interest. The cadet turned to him. "All right, Bob?"

"Thanks."

Now he stood alone again. "Well, that's what we've learnt. Bill's patrol was lucky to get there at the time it did, because it's far more satisfactory to get a fairly dependable picture of Blake withdrawing a lookout post because of the rising river than just to have gone there and found nothing. Also, we can take it that Blake's headquartered on the ridge across the river. My guess is he's at the other side of the ridge, astride the road. I suspect, too, that he's being lazy and concentrating his patrol work in the hill and river area where Bill saw him. I was prepared for the ford patrol to bump Blake and for Bill's patrol to see nothing. I thought it possible Blake would expect us to take the line of least resistance and go round the forest by the west track which leads from Khudabad to the ford, but it looks as if they've decided that would be a long sweat, or that it hadn't occurred to them at all. Therefore——"

He paused. He looked over their heads to the thorn tree under which Baksh still squatted, out of earshot. But Baksh was watching them. The muleteer squatted by his side and the guard stood bored beside them.

"Therefore, the ford is where we'll cross the river. We won't go near the Elephant Hill crossing. When we're over the other side we'll drive back along the centre ridge in two prongs, one along the line of the river and the other along the line of the ridge. That ought to bring us slap against Blake's flank."

He caught the eyes of the platoon commanders. "These are orders for the approach, then. We divide up now into an attacking force and a strongpoint force. Lawson will command the strongpoint force which will remain in this area, but up on the ridge and not here in the hollow. The idea of the strongpoint force is that it provides a rendezvous or rallying point for the returning attack force. In theory it stays here with the mules to accept an air drop this evening, then waits for us to come back tomorrow. In practice it will go on towards the river at the ford crossing first thing tomorrow morning. That's the longest way round, but it's a safer crossing for the mules and we'll rendezvous with them at the junction of the track and the road back to the school. Major Craig tells me that Sergeant Shaw will continue to umpire the strongpoint force, so that force will consist of Lawson, six men who are the weakest swimmers, the muleteer, his mule train, Sergeant Shaw—and Havildar Baksh.

"The attack force will consist of the rest of us. We'll start from here at 2200 hours tonight. If it's not clouded over there'll be a moon and that should help us in the ravine. The patrol says that in daylight it took them two and a half hours going as fast as they could. Double that time for darkness, the pace of the column compared with the pace of a patrol, and for the fact we'll be carrying three sections of raft. Five hours. We should be at the ford at 0300. I want to begin the crossing at first light so we'll have plenty of time.

"This morning's ford patrol will lead us in and we'll march 11, 10 and 12 platoons. We'll march on the basis of each man carrying fifty rounds of rifle ammunition. In theory we should go with the minimum equipment, because we'd leave it behind at the strongpoint, but in practice we can't. In addition to our own individual arms and equipment the river party assault will carry the four coils of manilla rope at present carried on the mules, the raft sections and binding cords. The river assault party will consist of twelve strong swimmers under 12 platoon commander, who will put his platoon under command of his

2 i.c., and twelve others, starting with the weakest of the swimmers in the attack force. The weaker swimmers will do the carrying so that the strong swimmers will conserve their energy. 12 platoon commander will make up his assault force by arrangements with 10 and 11 platoon commanders. The assault force will march behind 11 platoon."

Ramsay waited for a moment before continuing. "The crossing may be easy if the water level is no higher tomorrow morning than it was today. But we must be prepared to swim for it. If we have to swim for it the assault force will swim two ropes across, establish a covering party of twelve in the jungle on the opposite bank. One rope'll be used as a safety precaution for the good swimmers. The other rope'll be used to haul the raft across with the poor swimmers. We'll attach the third rope to the stern of the raft to haul it back for other trips. The idea of the raft is that you should hang on to it and not sit on it."

Someone said, "What's the fourth rope for, Bob?"

"The fourth rope's a spare in case one snaps."

"If a rope snaps we shan't need a spare!"

Ramsay said, "Once across, in theory we'd leave a guard on the raft. In practice we'll leave it there for the strongpoint force to salvage when they cross. That's about all, I think. Any questions?"

"Yes. What about some decent grub?"

There was a shout of approval. Ramsay's own hunger sharpened.

"In theory the strongpoint force gets this air-lift and has a hot meal going for us on our return. In practice I understand Sar-Major Thompson has special rations stocked up for us in Blake's area. That right, sir?"

Craig nodded, explained, "We've laid it on that the school would deliver our rations to Blake. As soon as we've finished tomorrow you should be able to tuck in."

A cadet asked, "Do we give Blake back his havildar?"

Another said, "Not till he's given Tony his socks back."

The laughter rippled through them. Tony said, "He can keep 'em. I don't wear socks any more." He slipped off an unlaced boot and waggled his foot in the air. The foot of the sock was worn away and the flesh beneath was red and puffed.

Ramsay called, "Right. That's all, then. If the platoon commanders will stay."

The men dragged themselves to their feet and gradually the hollow cleared and the afternoon grew still. For a while he discussed the night's plans with the platoon commanders and then they too went. Craig had gone, and Shaw, and he was alone again in the clear patch of scrub. Beyond, where Baksh squatted, Lawson talked to the muleteer, and Ramsay could see from Lawson's gestures that he pointed out to the man the way by which they would go in the morning and the way by which the attack force would go that night, and he looked from Lawson to Baksh and saw that Baksh listened.

Craig (5)

AT 23 15 hours, an hour and a quarter after they had set out down the ravine, Ramsay made a halt and sent his runner back along the column to call the platoon commanders forward. Craig said, "Is this where we wait?" and Ramsay nodded his head. A moon had climbed into the empty sky and hung above the ravine. In its light the shadows which men and trees cast appeared denser, more tangible than they, as though the picture of them were seen in negative. To Craig, Ramsay's face was a dark oval above a white throat, below a white topee.

Craig shivered, although the air was still warm from the day's sun. He could hear the life of the forest now that the sound of their movement through it had ended. Cigarette ends glowed down the line of the resting column. The thought came: In the night a man is more himself.

When the platoon commanders had come and Ramsay had told them why they had halted there was a moment or two of silence and in it Craig's doubts took shape. When the questions came they were questions Craig knew Ramsay's answers to, but questions which remained questions and, in the scrub, under the moon, would not be answered in Ramsay's way, or in his own way, for he had no way except to doubt.

"How long do we wait then, Bob?"

"Until 0100."

"But that only gives us two hours to get to the ford if Baksh doesn't escape and we have to carry on on this route."

"Why only two hours?"

"You gave 0300 as an ETA."

"0500 will do. And I don't think it'll take us another four hours' marching, the pace we're making."

"Suppose Baksh escapes after 0100 hours?"

"You're forgetting, Angus. If Baksh hasn't escaped by 0015 hours Lawson clamps down and makes sure he doesn't escape at all. He'll give him till then, but can't give him till later because we must move in one direction or another at 0100 and it'll take 'em up to three-quarters of an hour to get a message to us here."

"Who's bringing the message?"

"Lawson said he'd send two men, one of them a chap who patrolled this way this morning."

"That'll be Dawson."

"Suppose they get lost?"

"You can't get lost in this ravine."

"Baksh won't escape. He won't know the way to the river."

"There's a track. And he's a senior NCO, well trained."

"Perhaps he can't swim. If he can't swim he'll funk the river and go back to Lawson and then it'll be too late."

"He can swim."

"How d'you know?"

"Bob's right. Baksh said he could swim like a fish."

"That's right, Angus. When Bob asked us to classify swimmers at Khudabad, Lester tried to put the wind up Baksh like he did over the tiger, and Baksh said he was a good swimmer."

"Oh. Bob, did you know that, or were you taking a chance?"

"I knew that. It was one of the reasons I asked for a classification, to find out how well Baksh could swim."

"You mean you've planned this about Baksh from the beginning?"

"Almost from the beginning."

"Then the orders this afternoon were just eyewash?"

"Partly."

"You might have told us."

"If I'd told you you might have been tempted to tell some of the others and Baksh would have got to hear about it or sensed it. So I told nobody. Except the Chief Umpire."

They turned their dark faces to Craig. He said nothing, but waited for his doubts to go, as theirs had gone or were going. His own would not go. The questions began again.

"Suppose he *has* sensed it? Suppose he notices they're deliberately letting him escape?"

"It's a risk I'm taking, but I don't think it's much of a risk at all. If he's intent on escaping he's much more likely to be tickled pink at his own cunning than to suspect we're being cunning too."

"But look, Bob, say you're right, say he escapes, say he's escaped now. He could be back with Blake in, what? Two hours. That'd be about 0100. That'd give Blake four hours to get to the ford, get there before us, I mean."

"But that's where we want him to be. We'll be at Elephant Hill if Baksh escapes."

"Sorry. Sorry, Bob. It's pretty bloody confusing. I'll be frank and say straight out that I don't like it. It doesn't ring true."

Craig waited. He waited for Ramsay to say something that would make it ring true, that would make it seem as sound a plan here in the ravine as it had seemed in Khudabad, that would ease his doubts and remove the fear that had begun to eat into his marrow.

Ramsay said, "Of course it doesn't ring true. Nothing rings true until it's happened."

"What happens may be the wrong thing."

"What could happen that may be the wrong thing here?"

"The plan could misfire in some way. We could find Blake waiting for us at the Elephant Hill crossing."

"But we could find him waiting at the ford, too."

"The patrols said there was nobody at the ford, Bob."

"I know. But there might be someone at the ford now. There might be someone at the Elephant Hill crossing. We shan't know until we get there. We can't *know* what Blake's decided to do. We could have an easy crossing or a tough crossing, with or without the Baksh plan. It seems sensible to have a crack at making a situation that'll suit us."

"Bob's right. Anyway, the Baksh thing is laid on. We've got to wait and see how it turns out."

"Do we tell everybody?"

"Yes. We may have a long wait. They'd better know why they're waiting." As they were going he said, "I think we've got the jungle to ourselves, but Blake just might have a patrol out. So keep the chatter down, but don't stamp on the smoking. Until we get within a mile of the river I'd prefer us to act as if we're boss. From there onwards we'll have to prove it."

He lit a cigarette himself, turned to Craig, offered him one. Craig took it, fumbled for a light, then bent to the glowing end of Ramsay's cigarette, and as he did so Ramsay said, "It's all right, sir. Baksh has gone now."

Startled, Craig looked up at the dark shape of Ramsay's face. It was the moment for which the dream had so often prepared him, but the dream had played false. The reality was not that he should turn, but that he should look up, not that he should find Ramsay waiting for him, but that he should find himself waiting for Ramsay: not the Ramsay who knew Baksh had gone, but the Ramsay who had no means of knowing, who had given water to a man, carried the man's pack, come once to his tent to say, Do you disapprove?—the Ramsay who would not come again however long he waited. He felt the emptiness of his hands and turned away because for all their emptiness he could not bear in them the weight of all the things he had not given.

A few minutes after midnight two men came in with a message from Lawson that Baksh had gone. An hour later they began the march back along the ravine.

Ramsay (5)

HE HALTED the column on the last crest and went down the hill, followed by Craig and the platoon commanders. The rain seeped through the forest. There had been no moon this past two hours. As they went down the hill through the rain and the darkness he heard the strong voice of the river. It came to him like the sound of a long-drawn exhalation, a sustained sigh which came deeper than the sigh of the rain, and he understood that the river had a life of its own which it lived like a sleeping beast, curled into the shelter of the forest.

They came to the bank, stared at the dark water and the dark shape of the forest beyond. Ramsay knelt on one knee, bowed his head with eyes closed, then slowly opened his eyes and raised his head, watched the opposite bank, reached out with his mind to the idea of Blake so that if Blake were there his mind would lay hold of him in the way that a hand which groped in the darkness might lay hold of another hand. Slowly, patiently, he considered the land which lay beyond the river, pattern by pattern, alert for the pattern which did not fit, which would jar like the impact of a hand in the dark, and as he reached farther and farther beyond the line of the river, higher and higher up the hill, the sensation that he did so unchallenged communicated itself from mind to body and set his heart hammering.

Blake was not there. No impression or hint of Blake came down to him from the hill, no echo even of Blake from behind the hill. There was only an impression of the regular formations of tree and hill and of the way they stood silent, unliving, within the sound and the life of what the coming day would make them: the trees and the hills of a forest of which he would have his will, through which he would hunt Blake and destroy him.

He said, in a low tone, "It's worked," was aware again of

the men who were with him and then of the men gathered, sheepish, behind and above him, and he felt the great weight of them as if it were a weight he carried in his own flesh, the great weight of a body which was his own and not his own but the body he must carry over the river and up the hill, a blundering insensitive body with which somehow he must stalk the enemy. And then he remembered that Blake was also encumbered by such a body and at once the image faded and the image of himself as a pattern and of Blake as a pattern took shape again, but sharper, intenser than ever before, so that a kind of panic grew in him as he saw his own pattern clearly in all its separate parts, its tough limbs and its weak limbs, a chain-like pattern which had to be projected across the river, which had to expose, momentarily, each link, each facet of the whole image, to the mercy of the river, the curled beast which slept in the valley between the hills.

He rose, stiff-kneed. If he were alone, if Blake were alone, he could plunge into the river, fight it, beat it, find Blake, fight him, beat him, grant mercy or withhold it. Or Blake could find and beat him, destroy or spare him. There was a simplicity in that, a directness, an order, a sense of free choice. There was no simplicity in this other. He could not choose. He could not cross the river alone and Blake could not meet him alone. He and Blake were prisoners within the separate patterns of safety they had each devised and they had no choice now but to bring those patterns into conflict, no choice but to fight to keep their own pattern secure. I am one hundred men, he thought, but I am not in myself a man. There is nothing honourable in what I do. I am the heart of a machine that has no heart. I am one hundred links in a chain which is only the image of a chain. I must preserve the image of the chain. If the image is destroyed I am also destroyed. I am nothing without the image and the image is nothing without me.

He turned to his platoon commanders and said, "We'll cross in half an hour."

"You said it had worked. Did you mean about Baksh?"

"Yes."

They were silent.

He said, "We'll cross without opposition. Tell them to get

working on the raft and get the assault force down here with the ropes."

One of them said, "Is it deeper, d'you think?"

"Five feet in the middle, I'd say, judging by the height of the bank."

"You know this bit of the river, Bob?"

"Yes, I know this bit."

"Come on, then. Let's get cracking."

They went back up the hill, but in a moment he noticed Craig had stayed with him and he said aloud the thing he had been thinking. "John bodged the raft on purpose."

Craig said, "What?"

"John bodged the raft on purpose."

Craig was silent, so he repeated, "He bodged the raft. He knew what he was doing. He wanted to get rid of the weaklings."

Craig said, "It's something I've always refused even to think about."

"But you have thought it."

"No."

"You have thought it. If you haven't thought it you've known it." Ramsay hesitated. "Or if you haven't thought it or known it since you must have known it at the time. You must have known it when you saw the raft break up."

"Perhaps."

"And still you didn't have the nerve to shoot him."

"Would you?"

"Yes, I'd have shot him. I'd have shot the bastard."

Craig said, "Why? Because he'd murdered the men who drowned?"

"No. Because he'd murdered himself. He couldn't face up to the weak links. He broke the pattern deliberately. He broke his own image."

"I don't understand you, Ramsay."

Ramsay turned to stare at Craig because Craig had spoken so softly, like a man, he felt, weary beyond impatience, weary beyond all things because he understood none of them.

He said, "No. You don't understand. It should have been

your pattern and your image. You didn't face up to that. You left it to John and he couldn't face up to it either, when it came to it."

After a while Craig said, "Can you face up to it, Ramsay?"

And Ramsay said, "It's the one thing I've *got* to do."

As the man slipped the rope over his right shoulder the panic returned to Ramsay. He had to deliver this man, this link, to the river, but he saw how the river and the man himself might now evolve patterns of their own.

The rain had stopped and the dawn had already touched the sky above the river so that the water had texture and the forest had depth.

The man trod barefoot down the bank, entered the water and began the slow, fumbling walk over the unknown bed of the river, his arms held out at his sides. Gradually the water rose, hid his bare buttocks. He faltered, looked as though he had wished to lean into the stream and swim for it, but had remembered in time Ramsay's instructions to walk for as long as he could so that they might know the greatest depth they had to contend with.

He entered the stronger current in the middle and the flowing water broke frothily against his side, beneath his armpit. When he was in midstream he leaned more acutely to his left and the free rope swung out behind him to his right. The two men who held and paid it out drew it in to shorten it and ease the weight of its pull. The man in the river stood for a while leaning against the stream as though feeling with one foot the extent and nature of an obstacle on the river bed. Then he moved forward again and slowly the water level sank around his body.

They watched him scramble up the opposite bank. He turned, waved to them.

Another man now entered the water a yard or so upstream of the first rope. He, too, was naked and had a rope looped around his shoulder. When the water reached his rump he flung himself forward and swam. The current forced him towards the first rope and he grasped hold of it, paused for breath, then struck out diagonally to the current, fought it successfully and reached the other side. When he got out of the water he turned round and gave the thumbs-up signal. Then, separately, the two men made their awkward, barefoot way to the trees which had been selected, and in five minutes had made the two ropes secure, ten yards apart.

Ramsay caught the eye of the assault force commander. He said, "OK, Angus." He spoke very low. Angus nodded, signalled to the line of fully armed and clothed men and led them into the water along the line of the upstream rope. Ramsay watched them catch hold of the rope one by one as it came within reach of their upstretched arms.

One, two, three, four more links gone. Six, seven——

When the first dozen men were safely across Angus waved, indicated a fanning motion with his left arm. They disappeared into the forest.

Twelve men gone.

When the next twelve men had crossed six of them went into the jungle, six stayed on the bank by the upstream rope. The two men who had taken the ropes over now swam back for their clothes and arms. The six men on the upstream rope untied it from the tree and stood by its free end.

Ramsay looked over his shoulder.

"Bring the raft."

The raft, its three sections now lashed together with double poles beneath its bow and stern ends, was carried down the bank by its team. It was lowered on to the sloping ground and Ramsay inspected the lashings while the end of a third coil of manilla was attached to the stern.

"OK. Put her in."

As they bent to it he said, "Quiet as you can."

Four men entered the water, turned to take the weight of the raft, two to port, two to starboard. The upstream rope was fixed to a rope which ran along the bow end of the raft and then the raft was lowered into the arms of the four men in the water. On the opposite bank the six-man team pulled on the upstream rope until it drew the bow rope into a triangle, pulled again so that the raft moved away from the bank, ready to be loaded with packs.

The men in the water and the men waiting on the bank to

cross in the first wave looked at Ramsay. He nodded. The first wave of men entered the water one by one. The good swimmers put their packs on the raft, waded across to the downstream rope, rifles slung across their shoulders. Those who swam poorly waited by the raft.

Ramsay signalled to the team on the opposite bank. They lay on the rope. The raft moved, partly supported by, partly supporting the men who went with it. Before it reached the midstream current four men moved to its starboard side to counteract its downstream drift.

Twenty-four men on the far bank, six in midstream with the raft, six strung along the line of the downstream rope: three dozen of his force broken free.

He said to 10 platoon commander, "You're in charge this end. No more crossings till I give you the signal. Watch for it." He went down the bank, into the water between the two ropes. The water cut him in two. He leaned into it and began to swim. The press of the water in midstream was strong and he felt himself carried towards the downstream rope. He kicked more strongly against the strength of the current, defeated it, reached the far bank dead centre between the ropes. When he stood up his soaked clothes dragged as the water spilled out of them.

He looked at the bank he had left. The empty raft was completing its return journey. Along the bank on either side of the ropes he could see the men who covered the crossing. The morning light was like steel. Here and there it struck cold on rifle barrels.

He climbed the track, found Angus, knelt by his side and in a while when his breathing came more easily he said, low, "OK?"

"OK, Bob. Not a sign of them. They've all gone to the ford."

"Not all. There'll be some on the other side of this hill. I guess they're HQ'd there. Look out for dawn patrols."

"Shall I move forward?"

"Yes. Extend the arc. You've got thirty men now, and six on the bank to haul the rope. When we're all across I'll take Paddy's and Tony's platoons up river to get Blake in the rear, or meet him coming back from the ford. You and your platoon work up on to the ridge and surround their HQ area, but try not to get involved until you hear us firing, then go in and bust 'em."

"I'll get a couple of scouts up on the ridge now."

"Good."

"What do I do if we find nothing on the other side of it?"

"Establish yourself there and send a contact patrol to me. But you'll find 'em there all right."

"You see through trees, Bob."

Ramsay looked at the forest. It was dark and green, gentle with rain. The smell of it was in his own flesh, its whispering a singing in his blood. Angus said, "You've done a good job." He smiled. "Some of us hoped you wouldn't. We take that back."

Ramsay looked at him, but Angus turned his face away to watch the forest and the shadows for men who were not there.

Ramsay straightened up. His topee was still strapped to the pack which he had kept on his back for the swim. The rain water and the river water dripped from his hair and streaked his face. Now, more than ever before, he wanted to turn his back on the river and go up the hill alone, stealthily, secretly, holding the whole of himself to the shape of the body he walked with, swam with. But he turned back and went down the track to the river bank, and when he got to the edge he had a sensation of finality.

He gave the signal to continue the crossing.

The man who answered the signal was himself, the opposite bank a reflection of the bank on which he stood. The sagging downstream rope and the upstream rope with the raft moored on the other side were all that joined him to his reflection. As the men appeared on the bank and began to load the raft he felt himself stretched taut over the river: not himself, no longer a pattern even, but a tangle of disconnected lines and shapes to which somehow he must restore order.

When the men had loaded the raft they moved to the downstream rope, but some stayed with the raft as before. He had

seen it all in reverse. It was only a repetition; not even a
repetition. It was the previous crossing in a mirror.

He was shivering from the cold of his swim. There was
something wrong. The mirror was cracked. He said to himself: It's faster, much faster, take it easy, take it easy.

Confidence. They had confidence. There was a joy in it, a
carelessness as though they had broken free from him, as
though the river to which he consigned them destroyed their
dependence on him. He willed for himself the power to divide
the waters so that they could cross unharmed. He cried,
silently, I need them.

It happened when the raft was in midstream.

A man to the starboard of the raft missed his footing and
went under with a cry. To save him another man let go of the
raft and the raft swung out into the current and strained on its
ropes. The raft held fast, but the current carried the man down
to the other rope, brought him flailing against the men who
used the rope as a safety line. They yelled a warning, one of
them lost his hold. A man on the far bank splashed into the
water, another followed. They swam towards the struggling
group in midstream.

Ramsay floundered in. They were not men he went to save,
but links in the disrupted pattern without which the pattern
was lost for ever with the image of himself. He saw the mirror
cloud over and yelled, panic-stricken, "Get 'em out! Get 'em
out!" and the river around him became alive with the men
who answered his call.

When he began to swim he knew that he had swum already
to the limit of his body's endurance. The pack still weighed
him down. He struggled to the downstream rope, laid hold of a
body which heaved and spluttered. He held the rope with one
hand, shouted, "You're all right. You can stand, you can
stand." He saw the man's mouth pucker up, then open to take
in air, felt his grip become steady. He guided the man's hands
to the rope, watched him take hold of it. Behind the man, in
the middle of the stream, another man was trying to hold the
rope and hold the man who had lost his hold of it. Ramsay let
go of the rope to swim to them and at that moment the
current caught him.

All the power had gone out of his limbs. He surfaced once, struck feebly, knew that he was being carried by the river to the deep pool and the rocky ledge where once he had grazed his leg. There was a sensation of being whirled around and then a sharp pain where his leg was suddenly imprisoned, a sharper pain when he tried to twist himself free of it. For a time he struggled against the thing which held him. The forest and the river drew farther away from him. As the weight of panic and failure was expelled from his body the desire to struggle began to die, and when it had died he thought: But my image is not destroyed after all, I've won, I've beaten Blake: and he entered peacefully into the world which was himself, the world he had looked for and which, at the end, he knew no man could enter until the end.

Craig (6)

HE FOUND Ramsay's body where he had known it would be, trapped by the right leg in a fissure of the rocky ledge at the far end of the deep pool where the current met the fall from the hill stream.

When, secured by a rope, he had been down three times, a cadet said, "Let me come with you, sir," and this time he did not refuse. He sat on the bank, naked, shivering. He could not speak, but nodded his head, admitted his failure. He waited while the cadet undressed and secured a rope round his shoulder.

Craig said, "Mind the ledge. Keep to my left."

The cadet went in first and Craig followed. The water tugged at him. He raised his hand as a signal that he was going under. Below he could see nothing. The water was muddy-brown. Once he caught hold of a hand, was afraid because it was alive, unlike the hand of Ramsay that did not answer his pressure. The cadet kicked away and Craig could just distinguish his shape, felt the flick of his foot against his own left shoulder.

Then they both laid hold of Ramsay's body. He guided the cadet's hand down the length of Ramsay's leg until he could understand, through feel, the nature of its imprisonment. His lungs burst. He came to the surface and swirled round, grabbed the rope to save himself, felt it being drawn towards the bank. He cried, "No! No! We still haven't got him," and then there was blackness.

He came to on the bank where they had laid him and covered him with groundsheets. Their faces swam above him. He said, "Have you got Ramsay?"

"Not yet, sir."

"Who was that with me?"

"Everett, sir."

He tried to sit up but they would not let him.

"You've had it, sir. We'll get him out."

He watched them struggle on to the bank. They held Ramsay face down, two to each arm, the men in the water supporting the legs. When the legs were clear of the water he saw that they had had to tear the body away by force. The right boot and gaiter were missing, the trouser leg in tatters. The pack had gone and most of the tunic.

He said, "Bring him over here."

They brought the body and laid it face down. The right foot was twisted round. He knelt and turned it carefully so that it should lie more naturally. Then he straightened the right arm down the side of the body, bent the left arm and raised the head to rest it on the back of the left hand, facing right. He straddled the body, placed his palms in the small of the back, pressed down. Water gushed from the open mouth. He worked for twenty minutes while they looked on. Someone offered to take his place but he did not reply. In the end he got up stiffly.

A voice said: "Sergeant-Major Thompson's coming across, sir."

He turned towards the river. Thompson sat on the raft, was being hauled across. Some sepoys from Blake's company stood on the far bank with some of the cadets.

Craig said, "Tell him what happened."

A cadet went to intercept him, but someone said, "He knows, sir. Angus went to find him."

Later he could not avoid Thompson. Thompson came, looked down at the covered figure of Ramsay.

"We'd better take him across, sir."

"Later."

"They said it was only him, sir."

"Yes, Staff. Everyone else was saved. He saved one man."

They stood in silence over Ramsay and then Craig said, "Where's Lieutenant Blake?"

"He went off to the ford crossing. His havildar said that's where you were going. There's only a section left on the ridge."

"So Blake doesn't know."

"We've sent a message."

Craig said, "We'd better get over the river." He paused. "I'll stay for a bit. We'll bring Ramsay last."

Thompson saluted, turned away. In a while Craig was alone with the three platoon commanders and the body of Ramsay.

He said, "Better get on with the crossing. Leave a couple of men to help me."

One of them said, "We'd like to go with Ramsay, sir."

He looked at them. He said, "We'll take him together."

He sent one of them to watch the crossings and when he returned they lifted Ramsay and carried him down to the river. Two men had hauled the raft back and stood now, waist deep in water, holding the raft secure to the bank. The stern rope had already been untied, coiled and placed on the raft. The downstream rope had been dismantled. There was only the raft now, and the rope to haul it to the far bank. On this side the forest was empty, but on the opposite bank men stood silently to watch the last crossing.

Awkwardly they lowered the body on to the raft, covered it again with the groundsheet. As Craig and the three platoon commanders took up their positions on the starboard side of the raft the rain seemed to pause momentarily and then come down more heavily.

Craig raised his hand. The hauling rope lifted out of the river, cascaded water, took the strain.

Slowly, the raft began to move.

Craig (7)

THE DREAM had not gone out of him. As he climbed the hill the country opened, admitted light, yielded the secret of others climbing with him. The hill was safe, communicated warmth to them, happiness. Someone called, Have you found Ramsay, sir? and he replied, yes, turned to where Ramsay lay upon the raft which he and three others guided. One of them said, He's gone, sir, and then the dream grew shapeless, cold and dark. He cried out, Esther! Esther! and woke with the knowledge that she was not by his side.

Behind his shoulder the bedside light went on and her voice reached him. "I'm here, Colin." He twisted round, his eyes hurt by the glare, momentarily blind.

"I couldn't sleep," she said. "I was afraid of disturbing you."

She was sitting on the chair beside him. She had been near. In the darkness she had been near, anticipating his need. He lay back, eyes closed. He said, "Have I been asleep long?"

"About an hour."

"What time is it?"

"Half past three. I'll get you a drink."

"No, no."

Half past three. At five Hussein would bring tea. At the school the cadets would wake to the half-light of morning and the recollection of what they must come together to do: bury Ramsay with military honours.

Wide awake he said, "There'll be a Court of Inquiry."

"Yes, I know."

"What am I to tell them?"

"Only the truth."

"That I killed him?"

"But that wouldn't be true."

"It's the only way I can describe my responsibility. No one else will describe it. No one at the Court of Inquiry will blame me for killing Ramsay."

"It was an accident. He was drowned trying to save somebody else. You told me so."

Craig said, "He died trying to save himself."

"Himself?"

"His image. What he'd become. What I'd made him."

"What had you made him?"

"I don't know. I don't know." Then, "I thought I was helping him to be what I thought he had it in him to be, but he had other things in him as well and I let him destroy them."

"What things?"

"Things he needed. Things we all need." He could not speak of them, even to Esther. Spoken, they would only be words. He thought: None of the words we use is any good, none of the things we say truly reflects what we think or feel. The word forgiveness is an empty word, the word charity is a cold word, the word love can never describe the taste of it, the great hunger for it.

Esther said, "I need these things too, Colin."

For a moment he stared at her. Her head was bent, turned away from him as though she wept and would not have him know. And then a kind of passion grew in him, an understanding of their mutual trust, of guilt he need not bear alone because she would ask to share it, and with a sudden longing he raised the net, reached out for her. Without speaking she caught his hand, pressed it to her cheek as if to give him courage, take courage from him.

He said, "Forgive me, Esther," and she asked, "For what? For what?"